Maggie Bean Stays Afloat

TRICIA RAYBURN

ALADDIN MIX
NEW YORK   LONDON   TORONTO   SYDNEY

ALADDIN MIX
Simon & Schuster Children's Publishing Division
1230 Avenue of the Americas, New York, NY 10020
Text copyright © 2008 by Tricia Rayburn
All rights reserved, including the right of reproduction in whole or in part in any form.
ALADDIN MIX is a trademark of Simon & Schuster, Inc.
ALADDIN PAPERBACKS and related logo are registered trademarks of Simon & Schuster, Inc.
Designed by Christopher Grassi
The text of this book was set in Garamond.
Manufactured in the United States of America
First Aladdin Mix edition May 2008
10 9 8 7 6 5 4 3
Library of Congress Control Number 2007931953
ISBN-13: 978-1-4169-3347-2
ISBN-10: 1-4169-3347-6

For Kristin, my favorite house-hunting partner

1. Maggie Bean stood at the bubble-gum end of the candy aisle, biting her lip and carefully deciding which pack was going to help her survive the next seven days. Bubbilicious and Bubble Yum had tons of sugar, while Trident and Carefree had none, and were therefore the better, healthier options, but that didn't make the decision much easier. Paradise Punch and Ballistic Berry were off-limits, but that still left spearmint, peppermint, fresh mint, vanilla mint, wintergreen, and cinnamon. And the decision was especially important this week, because the flavor she chose was going to be the flavor that would forever remind her of the biggest, most important moment of her entire life—the one in which she finally revealed her true feelings to Peter Applewood.

"S'cuse me, miss," a sales clerk said, sounding slightly annoyed.

He stood just behind her, waiting to wheel a cart of SnackWell's cookies down the aisle. She apologized quickly and stepped aside to let him pass, feeling the familiar warmth creep across her cheeks. Bracing herself for unwanted snack suggestions, she held her breath and warily eyed the stack of green boxes as they moved before her. It wasn't until the sales clerk reached the end of the aisle and rounded a display of bottled water without another word that Maggie exhaled, and smiled.

It was like he didn't recognize her.

"Truth time, Mags."

Maggie laughed when Aimee flew around the corner and stopped short in front of her.

"Too round?"

"Too big," Maggie corrected, trying to find her best friend's turquoise eyes behind the enormous red sunglasses. "Unless the alien look is in this summer."

"That's what we'll find out tonight," Aimee said, holding out a stack of brightly colored magazines.

"*InStyle, Lucky, Seventeen, Glamour*," Maggie read, trying to quell the familiar pang in the bottom of her belly that grew at the sight of the thin, beautiful cover models. The sales clerk might not recognize her, but that didn't mean anyone else would recognize her as the girl she still wanted to be. "What about English, Earth Science, and Math?"

"Finals?" Aimee rested the alien sunglasses on top of her head to give Maggie a disapproving look. "You're really concerned about finals at a time like this?"

"I've just spent fifteen minutes considering the olfactory effects of chewing gum." Maggie sighed. "I think my priorities are in order."

"That's what I like to hear." Keeping the alien sunglasses on her head, Aimee tried on another pair. "How about these?"

"Perfect." Maggie stifled a giggle.

"Be serious," Aimee admonished. "At Camp Sound View, where everyone's forced to wear color-coded uniforms so as not to get distracted from arts, crafts, sports, and general summer merriment, the sunglasses you wear say who you are."

"Then I think we need more magazines," Maggie said seriously. "Unless who you are is a sixty-year-old woman hiding in a thirteen-year-old's body."

"*That* is why you're my best friend." Aimee pushed the white plastic sunglasses on top of the red ones still on her head, and peered past Maggie. "Everything okay here?"

And *that* was why Aimee was *her* best friend. She didn't have to turn around to know what Aimee inspected. It wasn't that long ago that Maggie lingered at the other end of the candy aisle—the chocolate end, home to Snickers, Kit Kats, M&M's and anything else that melted in her mouth and not in her hands (and definitely not off her hips). It wasn't until very recently, when she'd successfully managed walking by a ten-thousand-calorie bag of sugar without salivating, or thinking about how she could sneak it into her bedroom without anyone noticing, that she actually confessed to Aimee the countless afternoons she'd spent in that very aisle, selecting her weekly chocolate survival kit.

"Do you need these?" Aimee yanked both pairs of sunglasses from her head and held them toward Maggie. "They might help with the out of sight, out of mind thing. And remember, nose plugs are two aisles down, if the sweet scent becomes unbearable."

"I'm fine," Maggie promised. "Even if my senses were tempted—which they're not—my brain would ignore them, and I'd still be fine. I haven't tasted chocolate in ninety-three days, and now is definitely not the time to indulge."

"True," Aimee said, her concerned expression softening. "Because soon you'll have someone to indulge *with*. I'm thinking one hot-fudge sundae, two spoons? One chocolate milkshake, two straws? One brownie, two napkins? One—"

"Okay," Maggie interrupted, her cheeks turning red again at the thought of sharing anything with Peter Applewood. "Let's stick with sugar-free, zero-calorie gum for now, or my most thrilling dates will be with the Pound Patrollers scale."

Aimee grinned. "It's going to be so good, Mags. You and the captain of the baseball team. Should I grab a *Martha Stewart Weddings* before we go?"

Maggie shook her head as Aimee giggled and hurried from the aisle. She appreciated the optimism, but it made her stomach flip-flop, as though thinking positively would jinx everything.

Because the truth was, she needed all the luck she could get. That was why the chewing gum selection was so important. Her breath might not seem like a very big factor, but she thought that while she was pouring her heart out, showing her emotions for the first time ever, and telling Peter (in different words) that she thought about him all the time, that just standing next to him made her happy, and that she counted down the minutes until she'd see him again, it couldn't hurt if he was thinking, Wow, Maggie's breath is so *fresh.*

Deciding that, like studying, organizing, and planning

her future, it was better to over-prepare, Maggie dropped two packs of each sugar-free flavor into the red shopping basket.

Temporarily satisfied, she hurried from the candy aisle. Her mother would be done grocery shopping soon, and Maggie still had one more decision to make.

She waved to Aimee, who was wearing a different pair of sunglasses and pouting at her reflection in a display mirror, and quickly covered the length of the store. Hardly out of breath (a remarkable feat she'd appreciate later), she rounded a pyramid of toilet paper rolls.

And nearly choked when her breath caught in her throat.

Anabel Richards and Julia Swanson. They were too busy giggling and testing eye shadow colors on the tops of their hands to notice her, but Maggie recognized the Water Wings cocaptains immediately. Their long hair was still perfectly flat and frizz-free after a seven-hour school day, and their black leggings, long shirts, wide belts, and ballet flats were right off the runway. Maybe later, after she'd escaped from this paralyzing, embarrassing moment and was safe in her bedroom at home, she'd find comfort in the fact that they looked like clones who wouldn't know how to dress themselves without direction from fashion masters Marc Jacobs, Michael Kors, and Cynthia Rowley. Maybe she'd feel better that even though she wore boring jeans and a T-shirt, at least she'd decided to wear those boring jeans and T-shirt *herself*, because she felt comfortable in them, and not because someone else had told her they looked good.

But that was later. The only thing she'd find comfort in right then was disappearing, so she ducked her head, spun around, and hurried from the aisle.

Crouching behind the pyramid of toilet paper, Maggie focused on the happy Charmin bear and listened to Anabel and Julia laugh. Months had passed since they'd done everything in their power to keep Maggie off the synchronized swim team, and even though they'd kept their distance since, Maggie was still reminded of the girl she was then every time she saw them. Which was really unfortunate, since who she was then was someone she'd really like to forget. Or, better yet, pretend never even existed.

Maggie cringed as Anabel said something that made Julia howl in delight. How had she not heard them before she saw them? She'd read that things like this happened—that it was possible to get so caught up in a guy and your relationship with him that you just stopped paying attention as the rest of the world faded away—but she never, ever thought it'd happen to her. Especially since she didn't even have a relationship.

Yet. She didn't have a relationship *yet.* And she certainly wasn't going to get one hiding behind a thousand rolls of toilet paper.

"Hey." Maggie rounded the end of the aisle, grabbed two tubes of pink lip gloss, and pretended to examine their barely noticeable differences in color.

The giggling stopped. Maggie glanced up to see Anabel and Julia look at her, then at each other, with wide eyes and open mouths. A few months ago, they probably would've looked her up and down and made some sarcastic comment about how lip gloss looks better on people whose lips aren't totally swallowed by chubby cheeks. But now they looked nervous, as though Maggie had just caught them shoplifting, cheating, or doing something they shouldn't.

"That's a nice color," she finally offered when they didn't say anything, nodding to a case of turquoise eye shadow in Julia's hand. She actually didn't think it was a nice color—unless Julia was also buying a red sponge nose and polka-dotted clown shoes—and while she certainly wasn't a makeup expert, she'd read enough magazines to know that subtly enhancing your natural attributes was better than wiping them out with fluorescent colors. But, for some reason, she felt bad. Like they were uncomfortable, and she should try to help them feel better.

"Thanks," Julia said awkwardly.

"There you are!" Aimee exclaimed breathlessly, flying into the aisle.

"Here I am!" Maggie hoped Aimee noticed her exaggerated smile through the enormous green sunglasses she wore.

"Oh, hey," Aimee said, picking up on Maggie's warning the way only a best friend can. She pushed the sunglasses on top of her head and grabbed the lip gloss from Maggie's hand. "Oh, my goodness, he's going to love that!"

Maggie tried not to laugh as Julia's and Anabel's discomfort immediately gave way to curiosity.

"He?" Julie forced a smile like they were all great friends. "He *who*?"

"He, the most gorgeous boy you've ever seen in your *life*, who could be an Abercrombie model if he didn't find all that shallow materialism and superficiality totally nauseating. He, who surfs every morning, does the crossword puzzle with his grandmother every night, and volunteers at shelters —animal, homeless, you name it—every weekend. He, who totally worships Maggie and thinks she's his reason for being." Taking a breath, Aimee paused for dramatic effect.

"We'd tell you his name, but he's very shy," Maggie added, amused. She was pretty sure none of what Aimee had said about Peter Applewood was true—especially the worshipping part—but she certainly appreciated the shocked looks it brought to Anabel's and Julia's faces.

"Imagine that." Aimee shrugged. "Gorgeous, kind, *and* humble. What a combination."

Since Aimee could probably do this for hours, Maggie hooked one arm through hers and gently tugged her down the aisle.

"Would love to stay and chat," Aimee called over her shoulder, "but we don't want to keep Mr. Perfect waiting!"

They stifled their giggles until they reached the checkout counter in the front of the store.

"I don't know if that was necessary," Maggie said, unloading the tubes of lip gloss and packs of minty gum on the counter, "but it was definitely fun."

"Of course it was necessary!" Aimee dropped her sunglasses and magazines on the counter triumphantly. "For as long as we're friends—"

"Which is forever."

"Right. For as long as forever, those two will rue the day they messed with you."

Maggie's grin faltered as she watched the checkout woman ring up her purchases. Whatever happened with Anabel and Julia was a long time ago, and now she felt like a different person—a thinner, stronger, prettier person. But was that enough? Despite her new physique, fresh breath, and shiny lips, would Peter Applewood look at her after she confessed her feelings, and be happy she did? Or would he just be extremely uncomfortable that Maggie—thinner but still the same nerdy, boring, fat-on-the-inside Maggie—had put him in such an awkward position?

"Snickers are on sale."

Maggie's face flushed. "Excuse me?" she whispered.

"Snickers," the checkout woman repeated. She pushed Maggie's bag toward her, then reached over the counter to point to the small SALE! signs lining the rows of candy. "Three for a dollar."

And then, once again, she was fine. She was *not* the same nerdy, boring, fat-on-the-inside Maggie Bean. She was not the Maggie Bean who lived for hiding in her bedroom and consuming enough chocolate to feed a fleet of hungry trick-or-treaters every night. She was not the Maggie Bean who thought she'd never have a prom date, or fit into the black wrap all girls wear for their senior class portraits.

She was the new and improved Maggie Bean. And she was going to do her very best to convince Peter Applewood that she was the girl for him.

2. "What do you think the chances are of this being an abbreviated meeting?"

"With this meeting being the last time we're all gathered together to celebrate life, health, and our collective accomplishments?" Maggie asked without glancing up from her Earth Science textbook. "Slim to none."

"But what's the point?" Arnie groaned. "We've faced our fear of fat, fought sugar and won, and talked the whole process to death. Shouldn't we be rewarded with a few free minutes? Maybe I'd like to take some time to reflect on my own success by myself. And sit alone in a quiet garden and contemplate my past, present, and everything bright and sunny my future holds as a result of Pound Patrollers and all my hard work."

Maggie looked at Arnie. "You don't want to sit alone in a quiet garden."

"If said quiet garden has a PlayStation 3 and Guitar Hero, then yes. Yes, I do."

"But think of how disappointed everyone would be if you left even earlier than planned." Maggie lowered her voice. "I don't know if some people are emotionally prepared for that kind of heartbreak."

"Can you belicve it?"

Maggie smiled at Arnie before turning to greet the Pound Patroller who'd just taken the metal folding chair next to hers. "Hi, Samuel."

"This is the very last time we'll all be together like this," Samuel, the group's most enthusiastic participant, sniffed. "It all goes so quickly."

"What does?" Maggie's aunt Violetta asked cheerily, joining the group. She planted loud kisses on the tops of Maggie's and Arnie's heads before taking the chair on the other side of Samuel.

"Life," Samuel clarified dramatically. "Its stretches of time that might seem endless but that are over before you know it—before you've even had the chance to really process and appreciate every moment and its significance, before—"

"Do you think we'll get out early?" Arnie saved Samuel from emotional collapse as he leaned across Maggie to direct his question at Aunt Violetta.

"It's summer, people, not the end of the world."

Maggie giggled as Electra, their group leader, hurried toward the circle in a yellow velour tracksuit and blindingly white Nikes.

"So things will be a little different for a few months," Electra continued brightly. "So a few folding chairs will be empty each week because of various vacations, pool parties, and beach bonanzas. We'll all be fine, and we'll all come back."

"*Some* people will come back," Samuel said solemnly. "But others . . . "

Arnie and Maggie exchanged small smiles. They'd been counting down to this day—their very last Pound Patrollers meeting—for weeks. They'd done their time, achieved what they were supposed to, and were ready to graduate from the grown-up world of organized calorie counting and go back to being regular kids, just in time for summer vacation. But there was no denying the group's collective camaraderie, and despite their excitement to never return, they still felt bad that their departure might alter the group dynamic.

"We'll be fine," Electra repeated, winking at Maggie and Arnie. "Now let's get down to business. As you know, this is an especially crucial session. You are about to face barbecue upon barbecue of greasy cheeseburgers, fatty hot dogs, artery-clogging potato chips, and metabolism-wrecking strawberry shortcake with homemade whipped cream. Long, hot, humid days during which you'll want to do nothing but curl up with Netflix in your air-conditioned living room. Three months of temptation disguised as vacation that could potentially destroy everything you've achieved and put you right back where you started—or, worse, further behind."

The circle of fifteen grew suddenly quiet. As the other members exchanged nervous looks, Maggie turned slightly toward Arnie, who raised his eyebrows. As the Pound Patrollers leader for the past eight months, Electra had kept everyone on track, but always with an element of fun. Either she'd had some very difficult summer experiences herself, or didn't deal well with change.

"I'm kidding!" she declared, beaming after a stunned pause. "You guys rock. You know what you're doing, and how to take care of yourselves. In fact, I'm so not worried, I *encourage* you to indulge in a small slice of apple pie every now and then—you deserve it!"

"Did you do that just to keep me from crying?" Samuel asked as the group members exhaled and laughed in relief. His shocked expression was replaced by a sentimental frown.

"Sammy," Aunt Violetta said affectionately, flinging one arm across his shoulders and squeezing. "Get a grip."

"In honor of summer, and of everything we've accomplished as a group over the past several months, today we're going to celebrate," Electra continued before Samuel could protest. "And we'll get right to it—after one small order of business."

Maggie's heart tumbled in her chest as Electra stood and took her place next to the pink scale in the middle of the circle. Despite eight months of these meetings—meetings that she'd been, initially, absolutely mortified to attend but which she had come to actually look forward to as she got to know everyone—and her own personal success, Maggie still dreaded the public weekly weigh-in.

"Do you think anyone would notice if I lunged for the scale right now and threw it out the window?" Arnie whispered as the first Pound Patroller stepped onto the small platform.

Maggie giggled. She hated the weekly weigh-in, but Arnie would probably eat only celery forever rather than endure such torture. Their common aversion to the scale, their initial resistance to attending the meetings at all, and the fact that they were the two youngest members in their Pound Patrollers group were some of the many reasons why they'd become such good friends. Maggie knew that she'd never have survived the eight months without him.

"163!" Electra announced when the scale's metal bar stopped moving. She made some notes on her clipboard before beaming at the nervous Pound Patroller, and then the rest of the group. "Who wants to guess Mary's grand total?"

As the rest of the group called out numbers ranging from fifteen to fifty-five, Arnie leaned toward Maggie. "Doesn't look like I'll be tending the flowers of my private garden anytime soon."

"Our wonderful, hardworking Mary first came to us weighing 224," Electra declared loudly. "And after several months of hard work, dedication, and commitment, she's lost sixty-one pounds."

"You go, girl!" Aunt Violetta called out.

"Great performance," Samuel said, clapping, shaking his head in wonder, and jumping from his chair to give a standing ovation. "Truly inspiring."

Never one to volunteer to take to the scale and knowing this weigh-in would take even longer than usual as grand totals were calculated and everyone applauded, Maggie returned to her textbook. She'd resisted Pound Patrollers for months, and though she'd eventually warmed to the too-cheery meetings enough to not dread Wednesday every other day of the week, she was still ready for it to be done. It had served its purpose, and now she had better things to do. Like study for finals. And figure out if she should wear jeans or a skirt when she told Peter how she felt. Sandals or flip-flops. Tank top or T-shirt. Ponytail or—

"Peter's in."

Maggie grabbed the textbook as it suddenly slid from her lap. "In?" she asked casually.

"My house. This weekend. End-of-year extravaganza."

Arnie looked at her like she had two noses. They'd only been talking about the end-of-year extravaganza (with unabashed pizza consumption and marathon movie viewing) for weeks, and she sounded like she'd forgotten. Which was certainly the opposite of the truth, but Peter's confirmed attendance meant her plan was officially solidified, and that made her stomach turn—and textbooks fall from her lap, apparently. "Right." She nodded. "Great."

"You okay?" He looked at her, his eyes squinting slightly in concern.

"Of course." She patted her open textbook. "Big test."

"You study too much. The world is your classroom."

"Really? The same world you live in, with video games and TV on DVD?"

Shrugging as if to say it was her choice and there was nothing more he could do, Arnie turned his attention back to the scale, where Samuel stood on the small platform, wiping his eyes.

"217," Electra announced. "Which makes for a grand total of—"

"Seven pounds." Samuel sniffed. "Seven pounds in ten months. I couldn't have done it without you guys."

Maggie brought the textbook to her face to hide her smile, and didn't lower it until Samuel rejoined the circle. It was no secret that Samuel's love of Krispy Kreme doughnuts kept him on the slow track to weight loss. Maggie and Arnie had already decided he was a Pound Patrollers lifer. They even guessed that he gave in to his fried-dough cravings more often than not just because he loved the supportive social network.

Turning her attention back to finals, Maggie pulled a pink highlighter from her jeans pocket and started making notes, stopping only to clap with everyone else when a new weight-loss total was announced. She read, highlighted, and memorized until every Pound Patroller had stepped on the scale—every Pound Patroller but two.

"Arnie and Maggie."

"Ow," Maggie whispered loudly when Arnie elbowed her.

Ignoring her pout, Arnie stood and held out one hand. Maggie looked at his hand, then around to find everyone watching them with proud smiles. She capped her highlighter and closed her textbook sheepishly.

"Is this some kind of group thing?" Still holding out his hand, Arnie deflected attention from Maggie as she got herself together enough to stand. "Like on *Celebrity Fit Club*? Are you about to wheel out a monster-size scale for us both to stand on?"

"You two," Electra said warmly, holding out both arms.

Quickly sliding the textbook underneath her folding chair, Maggie took Arnie's hand and let him lead her to the center of the circle.

"Now, we all know how wonderful Maggie and Arnie are." Standing between them, Electra put her arms around their shoulders and squeezed. "We know how hard it is to gain and lose weight at any age, but to be their age, and sit with a bunch of adults every week when other kids are hanging out, having fun, and not worrying at all about the same kinds of things . . . well, that must be torture."

"Not at all," Maggie protested politely.

"It was a living nightmare," Arnie corrected.

"And for your reward—besides good health and a longer life, of course—I have an announcement."

"If I knew there were cash prizes, I would've started coming to these things years ago."

"This is way better than money, my friend." Still keeping her arm around his shoulders, Electra ruffled Arnie's hair.

"New car? Trip to Australia? Guest spot on *Heroes*?"

"I think everyone in this room will agree when I say that these two are inspirations," Electra said, addressing the group. "And to show my sincere appreciation for their time, commitment, and even their initial reluctance—because that was just one more thing they had to overcome to get where they are today—I have a very special offer for them."

"You really didn't have to get us—"

"T-shirts!" Arnie exclaimed when Aunt Violetta started toward them, modeling a purple T-shirt over her denim button-down and sashaying through the center of the circle like it was a fashion runway. "Sweet."

"www.PatrolThis.com?" Maggie read the back of Aunt Violetta's T-shirt when she spun around and sashayed in the other direction. "Patrol what?"

"Dude." Arnie's voice was heavy with disappointment. "You should've told me you were doing custom design. I have some amazing sketches of important *Lord of the Rings* symbols and—"

"The T-shirt isn't for wearing," Electra said. "Well, it is

because it's a shirt and what else would you do with it, but it's really much, much more than that."

Maggie leaned forward slightly to catch Arnie's eye. She didn't want to be suspicious, but this seemed rather complex for a reward.

"Because of your great accomplishments," Electra said proudly, "Pound Patrollers has invited me to head a brand-new, local program geared toward kids even younger than you. As we know, bad food habits can start at any age, and Pound Patrollers wants to reach kids in fun ways—including this new website—to get them excited about eating healthily."

"Wow," Arnie said slowly. "So Maggie and I basically started an entire weight-loss revolution through our own pain and suffering?"

"It's a very nice T-shirt," Maggie said appreciatively.

"I don't know about a revolution," Electra said, "but the company definitely took note of your accomplishments. And not only did they ask me to spearhead this new trial program, but they also asked if you two would like to be involved. They think you'd serve as great inspiration and motivation for other kids."

Not bothering to be subtle, Maggie leaned all the way forward to look at Arnie.

"What exactly does that mean, Electra?" Samuel asked when Maggie and Arnie remained too stunned to speak.

"Well, that's to be determined. There will definitely be a large technological component—kids surf the Internet more than they watch TV, so major efforts will be made on the website. The design is preliminary, but we're thinking message boards, fun, easy recipes, exciting exercise moves that can be done anywhere."

"You're asking us to run a Pound Patrollers website?" Arnie asked. "No offense to you, the company, or chubby little kids everywhere, but that sounds more like a job than a reward."

"You wouldn't exactly run it," Electra clarified. "You'd contribute, come up with new ideas for content, and communicate with website visitors on a regular basis. It's an incredibly exciting opportunity that can be done primarily over e-mail. Oh, and at one local Patrol This meeting each week, which you would help me run."

Maggie's head spun as the other Pound Patrollers started firing excited questions. Arnie was right—this did sound like a job—but Electra was also right. Maggie'd intended to never have anything to do with Pound Patrollers ever again after tonight, but she couldn't ignore that this offer really was an opportunity. Pound Patrollers was a legitimate company that was undertaking a new project with, she guessed, actual money behind it. Even if the trial program didn't last beyond the summer, and even if she and Arnie were compensated only in cheap T-shirts that they'd dust furniture with before wearing, it was still an impressive accomplishment that would bolster future Ivy League college applications. Contributing to a new business venture—even on a small, local scale—at thirteen years old was definitely way cooler than volunteering at an animal shelter (which she'd already done enough to include as an extracurricular activity).

Still, did she really want to be reminded every day of her summer vacation that, at one point, she'd attended Pound Patrollers for a reason? She might've achieved what she needed to, but she'd failed before that, which is why her father had sent her against her will. It wasn't her proudest moment, and it was one she thought she might like to pretend never existed.

"I'm in."

Maggie's chin dropped. "You're *what?*"

"In," Arnie repeated with a shrug.

She looked at him, eyes wide. "Don't we need a bit more information?"

"Mags," he said affectionately, "great achievement comes with great responsibility. And it's for the good of America's youth, which means it's for the good of America itself. A great country, without which we would simply be nomads looking for a warm place to lay our weary heads."

"This from the guy who wanted to wrap up the meeting as fast as possible so he could go play air guitar in his private garden?"

Apparently growing uncomfortable still occupying the small space between them, Electra pulled away gently. "We have some time," she said casually, "so why don't we talk more after the meeting? I'll answer all your questions and then you can decide after you're fully informed."

"Great idea." Arnie nodded.

"Perfect." Maggie crossed her arms and looked at the floor.

"In the meantime," Electra said, clapping her palms together, "you still have one last piece of old business to take care of."

Maggie looked up when no one spoke. "Not in any hurry to get on the scale for the good of America?"

Arnie grinned. "Ladies first."

Shaking her head, she couldn't help but laugh. They didn't always agree on his comedic timing, but he'd always been the best friend a girl could ask for in such circumstances. The thought was so reassuring, she headed for the scale without another word.

Just as she'd done every week for the past eight months, she stepped on the small platform and held her breath. There was no real reason to think that holding her breath would alter the scale's reading, and there wasn't even any real reason to fear the scale's reading the way she once had, but she held her breath, anyway, and waited as Electra slid the small weights along the metal bar.

"146."

Maggie grinned.

"You lost another pound this week, which means your grand total weight loss is . . ." Electra paused dramatically. "Forty pounds!"

Instead of immediately jumping off the scale and sprinting back to her chair the way she usually did, Maggie lingered on the platform and let the group's cheers and applause wash over her. She really was a different person from when she'd first started. She didn't know if Pound Patrollers could claim sole responsibility, but if the supportive environment had helped even a little bit, how could she not try to provide the same for other, younger kids, who would probably be even more nervous and embarrassed than she'd been?

Looking over her shoulder, she smiled at Arnie. He

clapped louder than everyone else, stopping only every now and then to put two fingers in his mouth and whistle.

If he was game for more Pound Patrollers—for the sake of America's youth, America itself, or free T-shirts—then she guessed she was too.

3. "Oh, good! Another dinner, another animal saved."

"It's not just another dinner," Summer corrected. "It's tofu and broccoli tossed in a spicy peanut sauce and served over long-grain brown rice."

"All organic," Maggie added.

"I'm sure it's delicious." Their dad stabbed a broccoli spear with his fork. "And I'm sure we can start our own wildlife refuge with all the chickens, cows, and pigs whose lives we're now putting before our own."

"You had salmon three days ago," their mom reminded him, coming into the dining room and pointedly placing a serving bowl of salad in front of his plate.

"Salmon is not a fat, juicy burger with extra cheese and bacon."

"Dad, please. You know this is for your own good."

He pouted playfully around a mouthful of lettuce, and Maggie grinned. It had been his last routine checkup—and high cholesterol—that had prompted the gradual shift from red meat. She was concerned for him, of course, but it wasn't that long ago that he'd made demands for *her* own good, including diets and mandatory Pound Patrollers meetings with Aunt Violetta, and she couldn't help but appreciate the role reversal.

"You even said you feel better," Summer added. "Not as tired."

"And you need all the energy you can get," her mom said suggestively.

"You win." He held up his hands in defeat. "I'm now and forever a fruity, nutty, granola guy."

"Because . . . ?"

Maggie exchanged glances with Summer as their parents exchanged small smiles. They'd been getting along much better in recent months, but Maggie still wasn't used to the grins, jokes, and subtle displays of affection. For a while, they couldn't even talk to each other without arguing about something. The fact that they actually seemed to talk now, even when no one else was around, when they didn't have to maintain the happy-parents appearance, was a very good sign.

"Because I got a promotion," he finally said proudly, taking her mom's hand.

Maggie had been chewing on a tofu cube, and focused on swallowing before she choked. "A promotion?" she squeaked.

"From sales associate to district manager of Ocean Vista Pools."

"But you've only been there a few months! That's huge."

"It *is*," her mom agreed when he shrugged modestly. "Your dad will be overseeing five stores and almost fifty employees."

"So you'll be, like, the *boss*," Summer said breathlessly, eyes wide.

"I'll be *a* boss, yes. And I'll certainly be busier, with more responsibilities, obligations, and challenges."

"But with time for at least one extracurricular activity."

Maggie watched another exchange of smiles. "Golf? Couples' tennis? Now that Dad's a head honcho, are you guys joining the leisure set?" she teased. "Arnie's parents are proud country club members. I'm sure they could get you a discount, and probably some argyle sweaters."

"Girls," their dad said, taking a deep breath and waiting for a nod from their mom before looking at them. "We're buying a house."

Their parents smiled expectantly as they waited for a response. Summer opened her mouth, presumably ready to squeal in excitement, but stayed quiet when Maggie didn't immediately react. Maggie knew Summer would wait for her to respond first, but she didn't quite know how she felt about the news. Her parents were the adults and should therefore know best, but her dad had just rejoined the workforce a few months ago after a very long hiatus and significant financial stress. It wasn't that long ago that they were eating boxed mashed potatoes for dinner because they were on sale and cheaper than real potatoes. She shoved a forkful of tofu, broccoli, and rice in her mouth and chewed thoughtfully. "We can do that?" she asked finally.

"It might take a little while. We have to find a house, first. And save a bit more for a down payment. But you know I worked as much overtime as I could during the past few months as the company grew and expanded to new locations, and the extra income allowed your mother and me to pay off some bills and put money aside every week. And this promotion came with a significant salary increase as well as a sizable bonus—summer is a pool company's craziest time, of course, so they wanted to make sure I felt good about things before the season got underway." He took a deep breath. "So, yes, we can. It won't be easy, but it's time."

A house. *Their* house. That they owned themselves, and could paint and decorate and call home. They'd always rented, and the one time they'd come close to buying, her dad had been laid off. That was right before they'd been forced to move into their current house—by far the cheapest, smallest, and least maintained of all she'd known—and her dad had wakened every day to watch daytime talk shows rather than find another job. Visions of lilac paint and frilly curtains swirled in her head, and she was about to give in to the excitement turning in her belly when another thought shattered her brief Martha Stewart moment. "Will we have to change schools?"

"Well—"

"No," Maggie interrupted before her mother could say anything she couldn't bear to hear. "No way."

"Mag Pie," her dad said gently. "We would love to keep you and Summer in your schools, and will do our very best to make that happen. But Lakeview Heights is a very expensive town. It's one thing to rent, and definitely another to buy."

"Then we just won't buy. At least not until Summer and I go to college. Then you can move to Alaska, if you want."

"Maggie, please try to understand. Buying a house is a very big investment and commitment, and while location is important, there are many, many other factors to consider."

"The surrounding towns are lovely, with very good schools," her dad added cheerily, oblivious to the fact that her mom had bit her lip and was watching him as he spoke, obviously nervous that he'd say too much. "And they're so close! You could still see Aimee after school, if you wanted."

After school? What about before first period, when they caught up on everything that had happened since their last phone call the night before? Or in gym, when they talked about which movie to see that weekend while pretending to shoot hoops? Or at lunch, when they observed their classmates for new couples, breakups, and everyone on the verge of either? And what about high school? There was no way she'd survive four years of college preparation and inevitable social drama without her best friend.

"Nothing's set in stone," her dad reassured Maggie when she slumped in her chair and stared glumly at the small mound of tofu and broccoli. "And who knows what we'll find once we start looking? But we just wanted you to know that we'll be exploring all options so we do what's best for the entire family."

"Can my room be green?"

Maggie watched her mother kiss the top of Summer's head gratefully.

"Your room can be green, pink, blue, orange, yellow, or any other color of the rainbow." She looked at Maggie. "Wherever it is, your room will be *your room*, and we won't stop shopping and decorating until it feels that way."

Maggie quickly shoved tofu cubes and broccoli spears in her mouth. Suddenly consumed by the need to leave the table, she chewed and swallowed without breathing. "Homework," she said around a wad of brown rice when her plate was clean.

Ignoring her parents' concerned looks, she deposited her dishes in the kitchen and hurried to her room. She closed the door, grabbed her iPod from her desk, and dropped to the floor. As her favorite techno workout mix pulsated in her ears, she lay on her back and shimmied across the rug until she felt the metal frame of her bed against her shins. Placing her hands behind her head, she lifted and lowered her torso, doing crunches in time to the thumping bass.

She knew buying a house was a big deal. She knew that simply being *able* to buy a house was big deal, and a huge accomplishment for her family. She knew both her parents had been working like crazy—especially her dad, who, whether he was trying to make up for lost time, prove to them that though he might've gotten sidetracked, he really did want to be a good husband and father, or a combination of both, had asked for and accepted any available extra work from his company to get to this point. She knew that she should be happy about all of it. And if her parents had sprung this on her at the beginning of the school year, when the highlight of every week had been stocking up on economy-size bags of Snickers and M&Ms that she devoured in her room at night, she probably would've been.

But this wasn't the beginning of the school year. This was the end. And a lot had happened in the months in between.

She did fifty crunches, restarted the "Sweat It Out" playlist and kept going, ignoring the burning in her abs. She lifted and lowered, and thought about when she and Aimee had tried out for the Water Wings on a whim last October. She thought about how she'd secretly dieted, exercised, and practiced for weeks beforehand, only to be shut out by the team's discriminating cocaptains for not fitting the perfect Barbie-body mold. She thought about how she'd cried in her Reese's Pieces for weeks afterward, packing back on every pound she'd lost, and losing any self-esteem she'd gained. She thought about how, when she finally emerged from her empty bag of candy, she'd found the cocaptains had been called out for their unfair judging and their wrongs righted in the form of invitations to join the Water Wings or the regular swim team. She thought about how she eventually chose the swim team over Water Wings so she could officially start over, and leave the drama of tryouts and turndowns behind. She thought about how amazing it felt to wear the swim team's sleek, black, racerback one-piece for the first time, and how, after spending hours in the pool every single day, perfecting her form and slashing seconds from her time, it came to feel like a second skin.

And she thought about the very first race she won. Not just finished—*won*. She thought about how she hadn't thought at all about winning while she was swimming, how she'd just focused on her form and breathing, how when she realized her fingers were the first fingers to touch the edge of the pool, she had to glance behind her to make sure she wasn't in the pool by herself. (She wasn't, and the eight other swimmers followed closely behind.) In a matter of a few months, and after a lot of hard work, she'd gone from eating candy under her covers, to doing Richard Simmons exercise tapes in the privacy of her bedroom, to competing in and *winning* an actual athletic event.

She lifted and lowered her torso until it felt like it'd rip in two if she lifted it once more, and then flopped on her back. When the pain in her midsection dulled to a mild throbbing, she gently rolled onto her stomach and pushed herself up from the floor. She shuffled to her bed, pushed her piles of

Tricia Rayburn

textbooks and notes aside, and sunk to the mattress.

Looking around her room, she realized that she'd never thought much about it before. Sure, it had been a suitable haven whenever she'd needed to escape—from her parents, or from life, in general—but couldn't any room with four fairly soundproof walls and a door that locked serve the same purpose? It wasn't even like it was that nice to look at; it was barely big enough for her twin bed, dresser, and desk, and painted a shade of yellow that her mother called "warm as sunshine" and "sweet as freshly squeezed lemonade on a hot summer day," but which more closely resembled honey mustard, or ginger ale. They couldn't change the color because they didn't own the house, so they'd brightened it up as best they could with white eyelet curtains, a fluffy white bedspread, and framed photos of tulips and daisies. Unfortunately, whatever good their minor decorative touches did was muted by the unidentifiable, preexisting, permanent stain in one corner of the beige carpet, the shelf-less closet, and the ancient heater baseboard that squealed on cooler days. And all of that might've been more bearable if not for the room's very worst feature: its one window, which actually allowed late-afternoon sunlight but which was so warped with age, it no longer opened. She didn't want to have to change schools, but fresh air would be nice.

But, still. For better or worse, despite its many faults, this was *her room*. This was where she did her homework and studied for tests. This was where she talked to Aimee and Arnie on the phone. This was where she hung her (dried) swim-team bathing suit and goggles from the corner of her desk chair, and looked at the uniform in awe every night. This was where she planned her future. A lot had happened in this room in the past year, and she wasn't ready to leave it.

Sighing, she rolled onto her side and stretched one arm to the floor for her laptop. She lifted it to the bed, opened it, and waited for Maggie's Master MultiTasker to fill the screen. She'd become so busy in recent months, she no longer updated the spreadsheet of grades and long-term and short-term goals as often as she once did, but she still found it comforting to look at and refer to every now and then. She clicked through a dozen different tabs at the bottom of the page and skimmed her countless straight A's, various exercise plans, weekly weight-loss amounts, and potential tactics to attract Peter Applewood's attention. When she reached her last update—the one she'd filled in quickly a few weeks ago, as though its recorded existence would ensure actual follow-through—her heart jumped to her throat.

TELL PETER APPLEWOOD THE TRUTH.

She closed the laptop and stared at the side of her nightstand. She'd added one more decorative touch in recent weeks, and though Martha Stewart would never have approved of Scotch-taped photocopies, she thought they made for the brightest spot in the whole room.

Maggie knew she could take Peter Applewood's yearbook pictures (his sixth- and seventh-grade solo shots, plus an assortment with the baseball team) anywhere and tape them to any wall of any room in any house, but she also knew there was no way he had her picture taped to his bedroom wall. So, if they moved, and if she didn't see him in school every day, he'd probably forget she ever existed. And if Peter Applewood forgot she existed, what good would fresh air be then?

4.

"I think I'm going to pass out."

"You're not going to pass out." Aimee took a small bottle of perfume from the pile of makeup cluttering the bathroom counter and fired three quick shots into the air. "Walk."

"Walk?" Maggie said meekly. She sat on the edge of the bathtub, elbows on her knees and head in her hands.

"Through the cloud." Aimee waved one arm through the air, as though stirring it to keep it fresh. "Quick, before it fades."

"Shouldn't I spray my wrists? Or my neck?"

"Only if you want to seduce *yourself* with the luscious, irresistible, aromatic effects of vanilla orchid."

"This is a bad idea." Maggie stood quickly and ignored

the wobbling in her knees as she closed her eyes and walked dutifully through the sweetened air. "This is perhaps the very worst idea I've ever had."

"What about Scooby Doo?"

Reaching the corner, Maggie opened her eyes just in time to see Aimee coming at her with a lip gloss wand. "Scooby who?"

"Third grade. Halloween. You were Scooby, I was Scrappy, and everyone teased us about trick-or-treating for Scooby snacks for months." Aimee filled in Maggie's lips carefully, then handed her a tissue.

"That wasn't my idea," Maggie said, blotting her lips obligingly.

"Yes, it was. I wanted to be a beautiful, magical, glittery unicorn that granted wishes and turned all I touched to diamonds, and you convinced me that being a small, orange talking dog was more original."

"Oh. Well, I was right." Maggie grinned as Aimee brushed her cheeks with blush. "Nobody would've teased you for being a beautiful, magical, glittery unicorn."

Stepping back, Aimee surveyed her work. "It was a bad idea."

"Maybe," Maggie relented. "But worse than this?"

Aimee gently tucked a stray lock of hair behind Maggie's

ear and leaned against the counter. "You don't have to do it."

"I know."

"Things can just stay exactly as they are, with you thinking about him every waking and sleeping hour and wondering if he's thinking about you the same way."

"Or at all, which would be great."

"*Or*, you can take a risk, put yourself out there, and find out."

"But, he's *Peter Applewood*."

Aimee raised one eyebrow.

"He's cute, and popular, and a baseball player. He could be with any girl he wanted. And I'm . . ." Maggie paused, searching for the most accurate self-description. "I'm *me*. Boring, ordinary Maggie Bean. Straight-A student and recovering chocoholic."

"Peter's cute, popular, and a baseball player. And he's also your friend. He cares about you."

"Yes, but—"

"And *you*," Aimee said, opening a powder compact and leaning toward her, "are Maggie Bean. Funny, smart, *beautiful* Maggie Bean."

She tried to look away from the small mirror, but Aimee's hand followed her face. Never wanting to acknowledge her rounded shape and the baggy sweats she tried to disguise it in,

Maggie had avoided her reflection for almost an entire year before seventh grade. But just like anytime she'd inspected her appearance since joining Pound Patrollers to lose weight before Water Wings tryouts, when she looked in the mirror then, she was surprisingly pleased. Thanks to Aimee's artistic touch, her brown eyes seemed bigger, warmer. Her skin looked flawless, her cheeks like she'd just come in from a day at the beach. And her personal favorite facial features, her dimples, were clear as day when she smiled. "You do good work," she said appreciatively.

"You know we have three other bathrooms!" Arnie tapped lightly on the door.

The blush on Maggie's cheeks disappeared as the rest of her face instantly inflamed red. Arnie and Peter had gone outside to shoot hoops while they waited for pizza to be delivered, and Maggie and Aimee had taken advantage of their temporary absence to prepare. Maggie needed this night to go as smoothly as possible, and emerging from the bathroom more dressed up than she'd arrived, with Aimee, was sure to attract unwanted attention and make her even more nervous.

"I know you guys are close, but you really don't have to share."

"*Relax,*" Aimee mouthed when Maggie's eyes grew wider

in panic. Grabbing a fluffy white towel from a nearby rack, she opened the bathroom door just enough to fit one arm through, and held out the towel. "Where's this from?"

"Um," Arnie said, clearly confused, "the shower door? And before that, the hall linen closet? And before *that*, probably the laundry room, which I'd be happy to show—"

"I meant," Aimee interrupted, pulling the towel in and sticking her head out the door opening, "what store?"

"Towels 'R' Us?"

Maggie smiled when she heard Peter snicker.

"So you don't know?"

"It's a plain white towel," Arnie said, his tone more serious when Aimee failed to appreciate his attempt at humor. "I'm sure you can get them anywhere."

"This isn't an ordinary white towel. This happens to be one of the softest, thickest, most luxurious white towels I've ever encountered, and we'd like to know where it's from because, as you know, Maggie's parents are house hunting, which means they'll eventually be decorating, which means they'll eventually need the best towels money can buy."

Arnie paused. "You're in there together because you're taking decorating notes?"

Maggie didn't have to see Aimee's face to know her lips

were set in a thin, tight line, and her eyes were staring at Arnie, unblinking.

"I'll ask my mother's decorator."

Maggie giggled behind her hand as Aimee waited for Arnie and Peter to head down the hallway before closing the door and tossing the towel on the counter.

"It's a nice towel." Aimee shrugged.

"Okay," Maggie said, facing the full-length mirror on the back of the bathroom door. "Are we sure this is it? The outfit I will forever remember as the one I was wearing when my entire life changed?"

"Jeans, black tank top, and silver-sequined flip-flops." Aimee nodded. "Yes. It's timelessly cute, and looks like you care, but not too much."

"Because you know I brought other pants, tops, skirts, and that strapless dress I wore to the swim team awards ceremony—"

"It's perfect."

Maggie turned sideways, then backward, and peered over her shoulder at her reflection.

"It looks great," Aimee whispered, knowing Maggie was inspecting her least favorite physical feature.

"Did I tell you these are size-eight jeans?" Maggie whispered back.

"Nope." Aimee winked. "Not even a dozen times. And check out those arms!"

Maggie faced forward and flexed her toned biceps. "Who knew actual muscle lived underneath the jiggle?" Lowering her arms, she gave herself one more once-over before turning away from the mirror.

"Just remember the 400-meter freestyle against Lakeland Junior High, when you were so nervous going against the district record-holder, you could barely get your goggles over your head. And the 100-meter butterfly against Glendale Middle School, when you had a cold and thought for sure you were going to come in last place. And the 200-meter backstroke, when that girl from Oakville Junior High drifted from her lane and accidentally knocked you in the head. You were so nervous every single time—"

"But I won," Maggie practically whispered.

"Every single time." Aimee smiled and put her hands on Maggie's shoulders. "It's time."

Unable to speak, Maggie nodded.

"It's *time*," Aimee said again, shaking Maggie gently as her face broke into a wide smile.

And it really was. Any hesitation she'd had about revealing her feelings to Peter then—and not some other time in the fuzzy, distant future, when maybe, for some reason, she'd feel more sure of herself—was squashed by the fact that this might be the only chance she had. If her parents were seriously considering buying a house in another town, and if she had to seriously prepare for the possibility that she might have to switch schools, then things would change. And if things changed, there was no way they'd ever be as good as they were right then. Plus, if all the stars actually aligned in a way that Peter shared her feelings, she wanted that established before the stars shifted. It'd be hard to stay a couple if they went to different schools, but it'd be impossible to make the very initial foray into coupledom after she'd already moved.

"Let's go." She bit into a piece of cinnamon gum.

Her head swirled as she followed Aimee out of the bathroom and down the hallway. She'd been nervous countless times over the past few months—listening for the buzzer to sound before every swim meet race, waiting for test, paper, and report card grades, and watching the metal bar balance during Pound Patrollers weigh-ins—but this was different. Normally, being nervous was only mildly physically uncomfortable as her heart raced and stomach flip-flopped. But being nervous on the verge of revealing her feelings to Peter Applewood affected every inch of her body. On top of the expected heart racing and stomach flip-flopping, her palms sweat, her face burned, her skin tingled, and her internal voice repeated, "Oh boy, oh boy, oh boy." It was hard to believe she'd ever been more nervous in her life, even while wearing a bathing suit in front of half the school during Water Wings tryouts—a truly mortifying moment that, up until this one, had held the title of Most Embarrassing Moment Ever, and still made her squirm whenever she thought about it.

They followed Peter's and Arnie's voices and stopped short just outside the kitchen. Despite her nerves, Maggie couldn't help but smile when Peter laughed at something Arnie said. He had a great laugh—higher pitched than his normal voice, and contagious—and she hoped that what she was about to do ensured them laughing together for months to come. Encouraged by the thought, she grabbed Aimee's hand and squeezed it gently.

She was ready.

"Arnie," Aimee said sweetly, shaking Maggie's hand gently before letting go and entering the kitchen. "You said you have three other bathrooms?"

Standing in the doorway, Maggie watched Aimee lean against the marble counter, where Arnie and Peter hovered over a steaming pepperoni pie.

"Yes," he said cautiously.

"Do you think you could show me their towels? Your mother's decorator clearly has exquisite taste, and I'd hate for Maggie's parents to make a rash decision without considering all options."

"Now?"

Without answering, Aimee looked at him expectantly.

"But the pizza's here," Arnie explained weakly. "And talk about exquisite. All cheesy and meaty, and smelling like heaven, and—"

"It's too hot. Your mouth will melt if you eat it now."

Maggie smiled apologetically when Arnie glanced at her for help. She knew Aimee's request didn't seem especially time sensitive, but hoped he simply chalked up her persistence to best-friend loyalty.

"Fine." Arnie cast one more longing look at the pizza before closing the box. "But this better not take long. Reheated grease is so not worth the calories."

Aimee's arm brushed lightly against Maggie's as they passed through the doorway, and Maggie clasped her hands behind her to keep from reaching out and yanking Aimee back in the kitchen. She knew that in order to do what she wanted to do, she needed to be alone with Peter. And being alone with Peter was one of the things she was most excited about when she imagined them as a couple. But besides the accidental between-class locker rendezvous, when they barely said hello while frantically looking for whichever books they'd forgotten, they hadn't really spent much time together without Aimee, Arnie, or a hundred swarming classmates. Which made this either the first time, or the first and last time.

"Thirsty?"

Nodding gratefully, Maggie forced her feet to shuffle away from the door and across the tiled floor. She took the water bottle he held toward her and, trying to look casual (but mostly because she was too nauseated to stand and speak at the same time), sat on a stool near the kitchen's enormous center island.

"Can't believe the time has finally come."

She'd taken a sip of water to be polite, and suddenly had to focus intently on the stainless-steel rooster clock above the stove to keep from snorting or spewing.

"It feels like we just started, doesn't it?"

"Started?" Maggie asked after managing to swallow without gagging.

"School." Effortlessly draining his water bottle in three long gulps, he sat on a stool on the other side of the island, directly across from her. "It feels like we just showed up for the first day, and now it's already summer."

"I know," she agreed, even though, for her, it had actually felt like the longest year in the history of time.

"Did you change?"

"Change?" Surprised at the seriousness of the question, Maggie looked directly at him, her eyes meeting his big, beautiful, blue eyes. "This year? Well, I guess you could say—"

"You grew an inch taller?" He grinned. "I meant your outfit."

She laughed. "Thanks for clarifying. And yes, I did. I went shopping this weekend, and Aimee asked me to model my purchases." The truth was, she'd gone shopping every weekend for the past two months in preparation for this very moment, but she and Aimee had decided that this explanation was far less frightening.

"You look nice. Cool shoes."

"Thanks." She fiddled with the water bottle in front of her. Aimee was the one who thought they'd better come up with a reason for her sudden wardrobe change; Maggie had simply assumed that because he was a boy, he wouldn't even notice. And not only had he noticed, he'd actually complimented her. Nowhere in the rulebook of teenage boys (which she'd mentally compiled after extensive magazine research) did it state that they appreciated such details, let alone vocalized their appreciation. That had to mean something. "I like your hat."

He took off the faded green baseball hat with the frayed brim and looked at it, presumably to make sure he was still wearing the same one he'd put on that morning.

"So, anyway," she said quickly. "It was a good year. I'm really glad we all got to be friends."

"Yeah." Sliding the hat back on, he smiled. "We had some fun."

"Definitely." She swallowed. "And I was actually wondering if you'd want to have more fun? And maybe hang out sometime?" Forcing herself to look at him, and not let on how embarrassed she already was that she'd spoken too quickly and didn't sound nearly as casual as she'd intended, she held her breath.

"Well, sure." He shrugged. "Now that school's over, we all can hang out even more."

We all. "Actually," she said, wishing she'd been initially clearer so she didn't have to correct his automatic assumption that she'd referred to their regular foursome, "I kind of meant just us. You and me."

"Oh."

"I mean, no big deal. I just thought maybe we could see a movie, or play miniature golf or something. But there's no reason we can't do those things with Aimee and Arnie, too. That'd be fun. That'd be great, really great. In fact—"

"Maggie."

She snapped her mouth shut, looked at him, and nearly melted. He was looking right at her, not for the nearest exit. He wasn't even squirming uncomfortably. Maybe she'd just surprised him. Maybe he'd just needed a second to absorb the good news. Maybe he was about to tell her that he'd thought the same—

"We're friends."

Or maybe he'd just needed a second to figure out the gentlest way to break her heart into a million little pieces.

"*Good* friends," he emphasized when she nodded without speaking.

"Absolutely."

"So." He sighed.

"I don't want things to be weird," she said, hoping to save them both from further embarrassment. "We can totally pretend this conversation never happened."

"I don't want to pretend it never happened. I'm flattered."

She wondered if he could see the outline of her heart physically sink to her stomach through her black tank top. Flattered? Not that there was really any question, but that definitely answered that. There was no chance.

"It's just…" He paused, his face a combination of thoughtful and concerned. "It's just not a good time."

"No problem, I totally understand." She stood suddenly.

"Maggie, really, I—"

"So I don't know the difference between Turkish and Egyptian cotton."

Maggie exhaled in relief and sank back to the stool as Arnie hurried into the kitchen, a panicked Aimee on his heels.

"I *do*, however, know the difference between pepperoni and sausage."

"I'm sorry," Aimee mouthed to Maggie when Arnie beelined to the marble counter and threw open the pizza box.

"Thank you," Maggie mouthed back, shaking her head slightly.

"Oh, my God," Arnie moaned around a mouthful of mozzarella and beef. "Mags, all your parents really need in their new house is the number to a good pizza place hanging next to the phone."

Maggie avoided Peter's concerned stare as she slid from the stool and grabbed a plate from the counter. Ignoring the pang of protest in the bottom of her stomach, she loaded two cheesy, greasy slices of pizza onto her plate and made sure to grab any stray pieces of pepperoni and sausage that slid off during the move.

She'd do a thousand crunches later if she had to. Right then, she didn't think she'd ever needed comfort food more.

5.

"Three bedrooms, two bathrooms, eat-in-kitchen, new appliances."

"Seven bedrooms, nine bathrooms, kitchen, dining room, formal living room, den, pool, spa, tennis court, and guest house." Summer nodded approvingly before drawing a big red circle around the newspaper listing. "That's more like it."

"Please," Maggie said from her uninvolved place on the couch. "There are four of us. What on earth would we do with all that space? And who would clean it?"

"The maid." Summer shrugged.

"Oh, right. The maid will clean, and the driver will make sure our Bentleys are all shiny and pretty before he takes us to Applebee's for dinner."

"And the pool man will make sure the water's never too warm or too cold, and the gardener will make sure we always have fresh flowers in the house, and the private chef will make sure Mom never has to cook another dinner, ever."

"While that all sounds lovely, and while I'm very proud of your very vivid, active imaginations," their mother said, looking up from a real estate brochure, "let's try to be realistic."

"A *helipad*!" Summer exclaimed, circling another listing. "Perfect."

Maggie rolled onto her back and resumed channel-surfing. She wasn't really watching television, just like she hadn't really been watching television all day every day for the past week— her first of summer vacation—but staring at people whose fictional lives seemed better, worse, or, at the very least, different from her real life, killed time the way nothing else did. Despite her commercial-infused haze, she knew there were probably more productive ways to wile away the hours, but the way she figured, if she was just being lazy, and not devouring bags of chocolate while being lazy, then she was still ahead of the game.

"Maggie, sweetie, we have a few more papers here if you want to help."

"I'm all set, thanks."

"Do you want to pick out furniture?" Summer offered, holding up a stack of Pottery Barn, Crate and Barrel, Ethan

Allen, and Restoration Hardware catalogs. "Or light fixtures or paint colors?" She added a Home Depot flyer to the pile.

"Nope. I'm good."

"Summer, sweetie, I made a great whole-wheat, low-sugar banana bread this morning. Why don't you go grab us a few pieces?"

"And some iced green tea?"

"Great idea."

Maggie was silently estimating the total value of a six-piece luggage set, home Jacuzzi, and new, cherry red Mustang for the final round of *The Price Is Right* when her mother plopped in the armchair next to the couch.

"Maggie."

"Mom."

"Do you want to talk about anything?"

Maggie shifted her eyes toward her mother without turning her head. "Not really."

"It's all going to be fine, you know. Your father and I want yours and your sister's input every step of the way. And wherever we end up, even if it's another school district, I know you're going to be very, very happy."

"Sounds great." She turned her attention back to Showcase Number Two. "Keep me posted."

Her mother paused. "Aren't you even a little excited? To have your own room, decorate it however you want, and know you won't have to leave it anytime soon because we don't have to worry about rent, or a lease?"

"Mom, it's fine," Maggie sighed. "Just let me know when I have to pack my bags." The truth was that she really didn't care either way. In fact, after being rejected in record time by Peter, switching schools so she didn't have to see him at their lockers every day—and be reminded that he didn't think of her as anything more than just another person to hang out with in group settings—was no longer the worst-case scenario. It wasn't like she had a choice, anyway, so she'd take everything as it came.

Her mother leaned over and, without taking it from its permanent place in Maggie's hand, pressed the remote.

"Hey!" Maggie protested when the television screen went black. "I've won both Showcases three days in a row. I'm going for a record."

"So I stopped by Sound View today to pick up Summer's uniform."

"And?" Maggie asked, immediately wary of her mother's sudden cheeriness.

"And I talked to the camp manager, who's very excited about this season. He said they did a lot of renovations to the facilities, and that they're introducing a bunch of new and exciting programs. I walked around a bit, and the place really looks great."

"Fantastic. I'm sure Summer will have a swell time."

"He said they do have one problem, though."

"Too many s'mores, too little time?"

"Too many campers, too few swim instructors. They had some people bail and are having a tough time finding help on such short notice."

Sitting up, Maggie looked at her mother. "I hope you didn't—"

"No, I didn't offer you up. At least, not officially."

"Good," Maggie said, leaning back and crossing her arms over her stomach. "Because I have a lot going on this summer. I don't even know that I'll have the time to swim myself, let alone teach others how to."

Her mother looked at her.

"What?"

"Maggie," her mother said, trying to be serious despite her obvious amusement. "Besides that new Pound Patrollers program, which, according to Electra and Aunt Violetta should only occupy a few hours a week, what do you have going on this summer?"

"Well," she began, wishing she'd actually made plans

beyond spending every waking minute with her new, non-existent boyfriend, "I have lots of reading to do, for one. All of Edith Wharton's works, to start, and then probably Ernest Hemingway and William Faulkner after that. Plus, I'm going into eighth grade, if you recall—next stop, high school and my entire future. I really need to start researching colleges and their specific requirements, and planning my long-term academic calendar accordingly. On top of which, it really wouldn't hurt me to volunteer again, maybe at the hospital or something. And *then*—"

"Maggie."

Wanting to come off as convincing as possible, Maggie forced herself to look at her mother.

"You're thirteen years old."

"Exactly. The clock's a-ticking."

"I admire your dedication, I really do. And I'm so proud of everything you've accomplished and plan to achieve. But, sweetie, you don't have to do it all today. Believe me, the time will come when you'll need to think about those things— about SATs and application deadlines and college tours. But right now, *especially* during summer vacation, you should just enjoy being thirteen."

Maggie bit back her retort, which was that she didn't think there was anything particularly enjoyable about being thirteen, and that really, the years between now and the rest of her life couldn't fly by fast enough.

"I know you've never been to camp, and that's probably a little intimidating. But how cool is it that you could start off in a position of authority?"

"No fair." Maggie pouted. "You know I love positions of authority."

"And Summer would be thrilled to have her big sister there, and you'd get to see Aimee every day. And since it's only a day camp, you'd still have plenty of time at night to catch up on your American literature classics—which you could have even more of, as the job pays. Not a lot, but certainly enough to add a few more books to your personal library."

Unsure what to think, Maggie stared glumly at the black television screen. While she was proud of her usual ambition, and hoped to resume it eventually, she knew there was no way her recent rejection-inspired depression would allow her mind the freedom to focus. How could she think of a future without Peter Applewood, anyway? Plus, she really did love being in the water, and knew that especially after last summer, when she was forty pounds heavier and pretended that skirted bathing suits actually disguised her belly, it would feel great to wear a regular bathing suit without worrying about everyone staring. Now, if anyone stared, it would be to learn from her demonstration of the crawl, sidestroke, or butterfly. Besides, what were her other options? Did she really want to break *The Price Is Right* home-viewing records? Or know what Regis and Kelly did each and every night? Did she really want to let a boy—even the most beautiful boy in the entire world, whom she still loved more than life itself—turn her into a lifeless couch potato and ruin her entire summer?

"Here we go." Summer came into the room and carefully placed a tray on the coffee table. "Whole-wheat, low-sugar banana bread and iced green tea."

Tossing the remote control from her lap, Maggie took a small piece of bread and chewed thoughtfully. If nothing else, she could certainly use the distraction. "So, Summer. What's this camp of yours like?"

6. "That's the soccer field where I scored the winning goal for Team Stingray. And that's the tennis court where I hit the ball so hard, I dented my racket. And that's the obstacle course that I can finish faster than any other camper my age—girl or boy."

"Wow," Maggie marveled, following Summer's finger as she pointed out each important landmark. "I had no idea you were Camp Sound View's MVP."

"Three years running," she said proudly. "There's Lulu!" Squealing, she sprinted across the lawn toward an unsuspecting girl with two long braids hanging down her back.

As Summer practically knocked over her friend in a very excited hug, Maggie turned toward her mother. "Why do I feel like this is just the practice round for switching schools in September?"

"What do you mean?" Bringing one hand to her forehead to shield her eyes from the sun, her mother scanned the clusters of kids and parents.

"I mean everyone knows everyone. And not only that, these very happy reunions indicate that everyone has known everyone for a very long time, and that they've been looking forward to seeing one another since last summer. That's ten long months of excited anticipation. How on earth can I compete with that? Who'll want to have lunch with the new girl?"

"You're here!"

Maggie looked behind her when a very tall, very cute, very official-looking guy seemed to rush in her direction. She'd barely turned back when he was standing in front of her and taking her hand.

"Thank you so much for filling in on such short notice," he said, smiling and pumping her hand up and down.

"It's no big—"

"It is too a big deal. Maggie Bean, the district's 400-meter freestyle record holder, dropped everything to be Camp Sound View's newest junior swim instructor. Normally, there'd be a whole hiring process complete with official swim test and evaluation. But given your sister's outstanding performance year after year, your mother's glowing recommendation, your school swim team credentials and, frankly, the emergency-like nature of our situation, I'm just going to have you jump in the lake for a quick go-round for our aquatics director."

"Go-round?"

"You know, doggy paddle, crawl—whatever it is you swim types do. As long as you can keep your head above water, we're thrilled to have you. Welcome to Camp Sound View!" Squeezing her hand once more, he spun on one sneaker and dashed across the field.

"That was Adam," her mother explained. "He's the camp director. Deals with a lot of kids, and drinks a lot of Red Bull."

"I guess that explains it."

"But, see? *He's* certainly excited to see the new girl."

"Great. The camp director is summer's teacher equivalent. If I sit with him in the cafeteria I'll be socially destroyed for the next three months."

"Mags!"

She'd seen Aimee two days ago, when she'd been forced to vacate the couch and go out for low-fat frozen yogurt, but Aimee ran at her now the way Summer had just rushed at Lulu. Bracing for impact, she held out her arms and took two steps backward when Aimee landed in them.

"I'm so happy you're here!"

"There's the camp nurse," her mother called over her shoulder as she started across the lawn. "I have to drop off your health forms. Be right back!"

"This place is crazy," Maggie said, squeezing Aimee tightly.

"It just looks like a lot of people because we're all crammed on one field. Once groups are assigned and everyone disperses, you can actually see the grass." She pulled away. "This is going to be so good for you, Mags. You'll see."

Maggie stopped her eyes from rolling. She really didn't enjoy when other people thought they knew what she needed more than she did, but Aimee meant well. When Maggie had finally filled her in on the events that took place while she barricaded Arnie in a bathroom and forced him to analyze the texture of terry cloth, Aimee had said absolutely everything a best friend should—like it was *his* loss, and maybe it wasn't right for now but it would be later, and it was okay to feel a little sad, and that Maggie was a beautiful, smart, talented girl who should have absolutely no regrets because if nothing else, Peter was just a warm-up for the main event that was sure to come.

"There are *so* many cute boys here," Aimee said, hooking

one arm through Maggie's and surveying the crowd. "By the end of the day, you'll be saying Peter Apple-*who*?"

But Maggie didn't want a main event.

"I can't wait to help you find the cutest cute boy for this summer," Maggie said. "But I'm done. Give me a habit and guitar, and call me Maria."

"You don't play the guitar."

"I might if I had one."

"You know Maria falls in love in *The Sound of Music*."

"I meant pre-governess, singing-in-the-hills Maria. Because after she makes the mistake of falling in love, they're forced to plot an elaborate plan to escape from the Nazis in the middle of the night. That's exactly the kind of aggravation I want to avoid."

"Okay, sweetie." Coming up from behind them, her mother wrapped her arms around their shoulders and kissed their cheeks. "I have to get to the office. Summer's already with her group. Do you want me to help you find where you should be before I go?"

"I'll take care of her, Mrs. Bean," Aimee offered.

"Okay, then." Her mother smiled. "Have a wonderful, fantastic, amazing time. I'll see you this afternoon."

Maggie turned slightly to watch her mother walk to the car, and wondered if she'd made a big mistake. She could've been home eating cereal and watching the *Today* show or *Saved by the Bell* in her pajamas. She wasn't a camp person. She'd never been a camp person. Her parents couldn't afford it when she was younger, and by the time they could, years later, she thought she was too old—and, eventually, too heavy. Who'd want to weave pot holders or go canoeing with the new, chubby girl when old friends were everywhere? And while she'd occasionally wanted to be a camp person, like every time Summer came home with various arts and crafts, bubbling about her friends and waterskiing around the lake, Maggie had accepted that just wasn't who she was.

"Welcome, everyone—"

Maggie turned back to see Adam the camp director standing on top of a picnic table, trying to get the crowd's attention with a faulty megaphone.

"We're so excited to be back in our favorite place in the world, with our favorite people in the world—"

"That's Tillie, Morgan, and Sonia." Ignoring Adam like everyone else was, Aimee waved to a circle of talking, giggling girls their age. "We've been in the same group for five years. You'll love them."

"Can't wait," Maggie said, hoping her voice didn't give away her mild jealousy. Aimee, like the hundreds of other campers swarming around, already had her group, her friends. They probably wouldn't even see each other except for Aimee's group's swim time. And then when they did, how weird would it be when Maggie was helping oversee campers—and, therefore, Aimee—with the other swim instructors?

"And that's Finn, Alex, and Carter."

Apparently, Aimee was comfortable enough that she didn't share Maggie's concerns. Maggie eyes followed the direction of Aimee's slight head tilt to a cluster of boys in matching orange Oakley sunglasses. They stood apart from the rest of their group, arms crossed over their chests, not talking.

"The place is crawling with cute boys, but they set the standard, and they know it."

"Good. Now that I know who they are, I can totally forget about them."

Aimee looked at her, eyes wide, as though it were breaking some sort of Camp Sound View rule to not want to know the Trio of Ego. *No boys,"* Maggie reminded her. She didn't care one bit what they looked like—they weren't worth the trouble.

Before Aimee could protest, two long, sharp whistles cut through the conversations buzzing across the field.

"Here's to you, Camp Sound View!" Adam yelled into the megaphone before pumping both fists in the air.

Maggie winced as the air filled with screams and cheers, Turning to joke about the less-than-original camp slogan, her chin dropped when she saw Aimee dashing toward Tillie, Morgan, and Sonia.

"Green shirts!"

Maggie shook her head.

"Green shirts!" Aimee yelled again, jogging backward. "That's the swim crew! See you soon! Have fun!"

Maggie spun around, suddenly noticing clear color divisions as campers gathered in their groups and moved to their first activities. Summer had worn a yellow T-shirt that morning, and now Maggie spotted her with a dozen other ten-year-olds wearing yellow T-shirts heading for a baseball diamond. A younger group in sky blue T-shirts shuffled toward an obstacle course. Other groups in purple, red, orange, pink, and teal T-shirts, led by counselors in white T-shirts with STAFF printed on their backs in big blue letters, migrated to tennis courts, basketball courts, yoga mats, the soccer field, and a log cabin whose sign hanging from the porch railing read ART IS LIFE.

The field was clearing quickly, and she was about to panic and hurry after Adam and two other clipboard-carrying, official-looking staff members for directions when she caught a flash of lime in the corner of her eye.

Three guys and two girls in green T-shirts with SWIM TO WIN printed on their backs in big white letters reached the woods at the edge of the field and started down a narrow trail.

Maggie sighed. She hated running. She hated everything about it—the competition, the sweat, the pressure on her knees and, most importantly, the fact that she was no good at it. There was only one thing in the entire world that she hated *more* than running, and that was not meeting other people's expectations. In this case, that meant being late, so she allowed herself one deep breath before sprinting across the lawn and down the trail.

"Are you okay?"

"Are you lost?"

"Can we help you?"

Maggie tried to smile around her panting as she emerged from the trail and forced her feet to cross the final distance across the sand. The swim crew had beaten her to the beach by minutes and stood in their bathing suits near a lifeguard station, concern clouding their faces as she approached. When Maggie didn't respond right away (because she couldn't, because of lack of oxygen), a tall girl with a long brown ponytail grabbed a first aid kit and stepped toward her.

"I'm fine," she finally managed, resisting the urge to double over and put her head between her knees.

"What group are you with, sweetie?" another girl with a short blond bob asked, flipping through pages on a clipboard. "We'll get you in the right place."

"I'm in the right place," Maggie said. "I'm here to win."

The three guys stopped fiddling with life preservers and kick boards and joined the girls in looking at her curiously.

"Swim to win?" she clarified meekly. "On your shirts?"

"Speaking of shirts…" The girl with the long brown ponytail eyed Maggie's white tank top.

"I'm Maggie Bean," she said before their suspicion caused them to whistle for camp security. "Adam just hired me last week to be a junior swim instructor. No uniform yet, but if you tell me where to go, I'll run right up and—"

"*You're* Maggie Bean?" Long Brown Ponytail's mouth fell open as she exchanged looks with Short Blond Bob. "But . . . you're a kid."

Maggie shrugged, unsure of what to make of that assessment. She guessed Long Brown Ponytail to be about seventeen, and the others around that or a year or two younger, but she didn't know why this was shocking news. "Yes?"

"But Adam said Maggie was a 400-meter freestyle-award winner with a flawless record."

"That's true."

"But how were you hired?"

"Adam was talking to my mom and said that you guys were one instructor short, and in a bind."

"So your mom got you the job. That's cute." Long Brown Ponytail laughed.

"I know it was fast, but—"

"Are you CPR-certified?" she asked, her smile vanishing.

"Well, no, but—"

"Have you ever taught swimming?"

"Not really, but—"

"Have you ever attended Camp Sound View?"

"Not exactly, but my sister—"

"Have you ever attended any camp, anywhere, ever?"

Maggie paused before shaking her head.

"Sweetie," Long Brown Ponytail said, her voice thick with artificial sugar as she grabbed a walkie-talkie from the lifeguard chair, "I know Adam meant well, but we take our jobs seriously. And if we entrusted just anyone off the street with our precious campers, we wouldn't be doing our jobs. I'm sorry you wasted your time, but I'm afraid we don't need you."

"Erin."

Long Brown Ponytail turned abruptly toward one of the guys, thumb poised just over the walkie-talkie button.

"We *could* use the help. And Adam's so stressed, letting her go might send him over the edge."

"Don't be ridiculous, Ben. She's younger than half the campers here, and with no experience. We all know what it takes to be a Camp Sound View swim instructor, and she clearly doesn't have it."

"Erin," Ben said again, cocking his head and giving her a small smile. "She's a *junior* swim instructor—she'd work alongside one of us. We can even have her help only with the youngest kids, if the age thing is that big an issue. Give her a chance."

Maggie watched this exchange, heart pounding in her ears. Part of her—the part that still wanted to be home eating cereal in her pajamas—wished Erin would hold firm in her decision to fire Maggie. The other part—the part that liked a challenge and to be the best at whatever she attempted—hoped that Ben's cute grin, freckles, and easy manner melted Erin into submission, so Maggie had the chance to prove her wrong.

"Fine." Erin tossed the walkie-talkie on the lifeguard chair and faced Maggie. "Twenty laps. Four each of crawl, sidestroke, backstroke, butterfly, and freestyle."

"Twenty—"

"If you can do that without stopping," Erin continued, cutting off Short Blond Bob, "we'll talk."

"Erin, don't you think that's a little extreme?" Ben asked as the other instructors exchanged looks that were a combination of surprised and amused.

"It's fine." Maggie walked closer to the water's edge. The roped swimming section wasn't any longer than the school pool. Twenty laps meant forty lengths, a qualifying test that seemed rather unnecessary to help teach little kids how to doggy-paddle, but was one she could pass. She looked at Erin over her shoulder. "Do I have a time to beat?"

When Erin consulted her clipboard instead of responding, and when the others chuckled, Maggie turned back to the water. She knew they were watching her, but she kicked off her sneakers and shed her socks, shorts, and tank top quickly and easily. If she'd been on the beach a year ago, in her skirted bathing suit, she never would've made it off the sand, preferring to remain fully clothed so that no one could see what was underneath. But she'd spent a lot of time in her bathing suit over the past year, and any discomfort she might've felt not looking like Jessica Simpson or Halle Berry was outweighed by the strength she felt in the water.

Besides, since she'd sworn off boys, she no longer had to

care what they thought of how she looked. That was going to make life much easier, in general.

The Sound View Lake water was colder than the pool she was used to (though still not as frigid as Mud Puddle Lake had been last October, when she'd trained for Water Wings tryouts), so she waded until it was deep enough, and then dove underneath. Resurfacing, she started paddling out to warm up and loosen her muscles. When she'd swum far enough out that she could still feel sand if she lowered her feet (reassuring since, unlike the nice, clean, chlorinated pool, she couldn't see the bottom), she paddled to one end of the roped section. She glanced at the shore and saw Erin watching from the water's edge, arms crossed over her stomach, whistle dangling from one clenched hand. The other instructors looked up occasionally as they inflated inner tubes and beach balls.

The audience was intimidating, but not nearly as much as the enormous red numbers on the school pool's clock. No one timed her now; she simply had to complete the laps in proper form.

She started with the crawl, her arms and legs cutting through the water easily. The hardest part, she quickly found, was not rushing. She was used to propelling her body as fast as physically possible—and sometimes faster—but if she propelled now, she'd peter out by the fifth lap. Trying to keep her mind off of her body, she started mentally listing every state in the country, alphabetically.

Alabama. Breath. *Alaska.* Breath. *Arizona.* Breath.

By the time she reached Wyoming, she was only on her third lap. Rewinding back to the beginning of the alphabet, she began mentally listing every state's capital.

Montgomery. Breath. *Juneau.* Breath. *Phoenix.* Breath.

She still had a ways to go when she got to Cheyenne, so she switched to French verbs. Then prime numbers. Then the periodic table of elements, which she hadn't even learned in school yet, but which she'd memorized the summer before, just for fun. Then major events in global history. Around lap fifteen, when her muscles started to fatigue, she lightened things up with her favorite characters in American literature. Then classical composers, fashion designers, and exotic places she planned to visit when she was a millionaire. By the twentieth lap, she was on Will Ferrell movies.

Elf. Breath. *Talladega Nights.* Breath. *Blades of Glory.* Breath.

When she reached the rope for the last time, she was tempted to take a minute to rest before heading for shore, but didn't want to give Erin any reason to fault her. She'd just met her, but Maggie could already hear her cool voice scolding, "Sure, you finished twenty laps—but you needed to *relax* afterward. There's no time for relaxing when you're responsible for hundreds of precious Sound View campers!" So, when she reached the rope for the last time, she immediately turned and paddled inland without breaking her pace. She even jogged through the water when it became too shallow to swim.

The first groups had arrived by the time she reached the beach, and the swim instructors were occupied with attendance and organization. Erin had been watching Maggie's every move, but now talked and laughed with a group counselor as though she were far too busy to have been paying close attention. Happy for the moment to herself, Maggie grabbed her towel from her backpack and began drying off.

"Hey."

Maggie glanced up to see Ben passing by, carrying one little boy and following a dozen others as they raced toward the water.

"I think you got the job."

Maggie returned his smile and watched him hurry after his group. As the little boys bounded in the water, dunking, splashing, yelling, and laughing, Ben stood at the water's edge, talking quietly with the little boy he still carried. If Maggie hadn't sworn off cute boys forever, she might've appreciated Ben's dark curly hair, his height (around six feet one, she guessed), and his sensitivity, which was obvious in the way he interacted with the shy camper clinging to his shoulders. But since she had, she pulled shorts on over her damp swimsuit, walked over to Erin, and waited for her to finish the school year recap with the group counselor.

"Your stamina's decent and your form's okay," Erin finally said, flipping through pages on her clipboard instead of looking at Maggie after the counselor had rejoined her group.

Based on Erin's reluctance to admit them, Maggie guessed those assessments were understatements.

"You don't know anything about camp policies or procedures, and I for one don't have time to teach you." Reaching the last of her stack of papers, she flipped back to the beginning, hugged the clipboard to her chest, and eyed Maggie through dark sunglasses. "But your uniform's in the main office. Don't forget the whistle."

7.

"How did we get here?"

"Well," Arnie said, joining Maggie at the front of the Lakeview Elementary School classroom, "your mom dropped you off in a Toyota Camry, and my nanny—"

"I know how we got here *physically*." Maggie patted his back in mock appreciation. "But how did we become weight-loss role models?"

"You know that goofy guy in the SUBWAY commercials? The one who lost hundreds of pounds living on two sandwiches and diet soda every day?"

Maggie nodded.

"We're the Pound Patrollers version of him. Minus the endorsement deal, tons of money, and a lifetime supply of chicken teriyaki on whole wheat."

"We were *so* robbed."

"Oh, goodie! You're both here!" Electra burst through the classroom door, a blur of turquoise velour. "We have oodles to do before the kids arrive."

"What's all this?" Maggie asked as Electra unloaded posters, papers, vegetable cutouts, and DVDs onto a desk.

"Ammo."

"Ammo?" Arnie repeated, amused. "That doesn't sound very kid-friendly."

"It's not for the kids," Electra said, unrolling an enormous food pyramid poster. "It's for the parents."

"Parents?" Always the good, responsible friend, Maggie'd never had a problem with anyone's parents, but her pulse quickened, anyway.

"It's the first meeting of a brand-new trial program. Good parents will want to make sure we're doing our jobs and that they're getting what they paid for."

"Okay, I'm no expert—though I am a formerly chubby kid with parents—but there's no way I'd want to come here if my parents were making me, and especially not if they were coming *with* me."

Electra handed Arnie a picture of broccoli and a roll of Scotch tape and motioned to the blackboard. "No one said it was going to be easy."

"Remember the T-shirts," Maggie said quietly, holding

the tape dispenser while Arnie hung the paper vegetable. She agreed with him, but this was their first meeting. They didn't know what to expect, and even if she didn't think it would work well, she was glad that Electra had a plan.

"Electra." Arnie's voice was alarmed as he turned away from the blackboard. "We love you, but I'm beginning to wonder if the stork dropped you to the ground already an adult."

"He means that as respectfully as possible."

Electra wheeled the tall metal scale behind the teacher's desk. "It's a weight-loss program. We have to chart their progress somehow."

It was clear their opinions weren't about to change the meeting's agenda, so Maggie handed Arnie a pile of cardboard fruit and gathered enough cardboard vegetables to make a cardboard salad. They split up and began covering the classroom walls with produce. When Maggie reached the bottom of her stack, she returned to the front of the classroom and watched Arnie juggle a cluster of cardboard grapes and a cardboard orange. Since she'd sworn off boys she couldn't really pay attention (not that Arnie really counted as a boy, since he was one of her best friends), but she couldn't help but appreciate how cute he was. He'd always been cute, even when hiding in hooded sweatshirts and baggy pants, but Pound Patrollers had been good to him, too—at their last meeting he'd weighed in at 170, nearly fifty pounds less than when he'd started. And the summer heat probably had something to do with it, but he'd recently traded in his uniform of hooded sweatshirts and baggy pants for colorful polos and baggy shorts. Also, "Did you put stuff in your hair?"

Dropping the cardboard orange, his face turned pink. "Maybe."

"You know the girls here won't be older than ten." She grinned.

"They're coming!" Electra announced excitedly, emptying a Tupperware container of real, sliced fruit into a serving bowl and adding it to a table of healthy snacks.

Not wanting the kids to feel uncomfortable as they entered the classroom, Maggie focused on filling paper cups with water. Aunt Violetta had basically dragged her kicking and screaming into her first Pound Patrollers meeting, and once inside, she'd done her best to pretend she was anywhere else. It had even taken a few meetings of hiding in the back of the room before she'd actually joined the circle and participated. She was pretty sure these kids had been dreading today for weeks, and that they would prefer it if no one called attention to the fact that they were there.

"Welcome, welcome!" Electra sang as a mother-son team entered the room. "We're so glad you're here!"

"Want to make a bet on how many kids we make cry today?" Arnie whispered, coming up next to her.

"Are you wearing cologne, too?" she teased, suddenly surrounded by a cloud of woodsy scents and warm spices.

"Focus, please."

Done filling cups with water, Maggie followed Arnie to the front of the room. They stood in front of the blackboard and watched Electra greet parents, smile too widely at kids, and hand them all sparkly PATROL THIS! buttons. After eight very frightened children and their cheerful parents took seats around the room, Electra closed the door and clapped her hands.

"Welcome, everyone, to the very first meeting of Patrol This, or Pound Patrollers for kids. We're going to have tons of fun today, and will get right to it after completing just one small order of business."

"What's with the voice?" Arnie asked quietly. "And why isn't she blinking?"

"More importantly," Maggie whispered back, watching Electra tuck a clipboard under one arm and push the scale toward the center of the room, "where is she going with that?"

"Okay," Electra said, consulting the clipboard, "it looks like Matthew's up first."

"Oh, no," Maggie moaned quietly. A little boy with red hair and freckles, who couldn't have been more than six years old, leaped from his seat, jumped in his mother's lap, and buried his face in her neck.

"Don't be nervous, little guy!"

Maggie looked at Arnie. She knew Electra meant to be encouraging, but she sounded more like a doctor with poor bedside manners about to give a shot. Even worse, the nervous tension in her voice and lack of blinking made her seem like Dr. Jekyll with poor bedside manners about to give a shot.

"Sweetie," Matthew's mother coaxed, "it's okay. We just have to find out how much you weigh so we know exactly how much you need to lose."

"Wow," Arnie muttered. "Parents should really have to take some kind of test before they get the keys to the stroller."

"Why don't we start with someone else?" Electra suggested brightly. "Lucy, would you like to step on the pretty scale?"

"And weight-loss counselors should really remember who they're dealing with," Maggie marveled. Pretty scale?

The gray metal contraption was more intimidating than the Camp Sound View obstacle course.

When Lucy's eyes filled with tears, Electra continued down the list of eight children. Not surprisingly, no one wanted to step on the pretty scale.

"Maybe we should all get to know each another first," Electra suggested. "Who here likes candy?"

Maggie grabbed Arnie's arm. What was Electra *doing*? Had eight years of leading adult Pound Patrollers taught her nothing about overeaters? And these kids weren't dumb. Their parents had signed them up for weight-loss meetings instead of swimming lessons, tennis lessons, or some other form of summer fun. They already knew why they were there, and Maggie didn't understand why Electra thought calling even more attention to that fact was a good idea.

When no one admitted to liking candy, Electra moved on to a fact-filled lesson about food groups and the very important roles they play in our lives.

Maggie leaned against the blackboard, crossed her arms over her chest, and watched Electra's audience. Her extensive knowledge of complex carbohydrates had already won over the parents, who nodded and squinted as they listened, but it was completely lost on the kids. Of the eight, half sat in their parent's lap, quietly staring out the window, and the other half squirmed in their seat, waiting for the chance to bolt.

Where was Electra's gentle humor? Her encouraging words that motivated without embarrassing? Her ability to make you feel comfortable no matter how uncomfortable the circumstances? Was it the pressure of a completely new program? The fact that she seemed more concerned with pleasing the parents than affecting the kids?

Maggie wasn't sure, but one thing was becoming very clear: Patrol This might have started as a great college application addition, but now, after just ten minutes, it had turned into something much bigger. Like Maggie not that long ago, these kids were uncomfortable in their own skin. And if their parents and Electra couldn't reach them, then she and Arnie were no longer just pretty faces behind Pound Patrollers' success stories.

These kids needed them.

8.

"I think I'm underdressed." Maggie watched her mother lean toward the bathroom mirror and put on a second layer of mascara. She wore crisp white pants, a navy blue camisole, and matching navy blue heels. On the counter lay a lightweight white jacket. In the summer, the only things her mother ever wore outside of work were khaki shorts and T-shirts. It wasn't like they were going to Target for cleaning supplies, but the coordinated outfit still came as a surprise.

"You look fantastic," her mother said, glancing at Maggie's reflection in the mirror.

Standing in the doorway, Maggie looked down at her denim skirt, red polo, and flip-flops.

"You don't have to convince anyone that you're a serious potential buyer." Her mother grabbed the jacket from the counter, turned toward Maggie, and kissed her forehead. "That's my job. Your job is to give me your honest opinion every step of the way."

"Let Operation House Hunt begin," Summer announced, squeezing next to Maggie in the doorway. "I've got notebooks, pens, highlighters, a digital camera, and an extensive P.A. checklist."

"P.A. checklist?"

"Preferred Amenities," Summer clarified. "Fireplace, hot tub, stainless-steel appliances, in-ground pool, central air... you know, the basics."

"Let's go, girls," their mother said, waving them from the bathroom doorway. "Wilma has a lot lined up for us today, and we can't be late."

"I wish Dad was coming," Summer said, sliding her backpack of house evaluation materials onto her shoulders.

"So do I," their mother called as she hurried to the kitchen for her purse and car keys. "But if he was coming that would mean he wasn't working, and right now, working is more important. He trusts us to narrow down the choices, and then he'll see the best of the best."

Hurrying after them, Maggie thought about how she, too, wished their dad were coming. It had been a rough year for them, and when he was unemployed and watching television instead of trying to find another job, they were either not speaking or fighting. But just like Maggie had come a long way in the past few months, so had her dad. Even before his most recent promotion, he'd already earned several bonuses at Ocean Vista Pools. He seemed happier now than she'd ever seen him—he actually took their mother to the movies every now and then, and occasionally brought home small gifts for Summer (crayons and coloring books) and Maggie (CDs and regular books). They were like a real family now, and since house hunting was a rather family-like thing to do, it really was too bad he couldn't join them.

"I'm surprised you didn't rent a car for the day," Maggie joked when they reached her mother's decade-old rusty Toyota Camry. As their financial situation had gradually improved, her mother had talked about buying a newer car, but they'd decided to save all extra money for a house down payment. The Camry drove fine, but with its rust-lined doors, dings, scratches, and peeling paint, it looked like a pre–*Pimp My Ride* project.

"Your father talked me out of it," her mother said seriously, sliding in the car carefully to avoid dirtying her white pants.

As they pulled out of the driveway, Summer took a notebook from her backpack and uncapped a pen. "So let's go over a few things before we get started. What should we be looking for today? What sorts of things will affect our decision?"

Their mother smiled at Summer in the rearview mirror. "Do you know how cute you are?"

"Mom. We really don't have time for that."

"Sorry." Shifting her eyes back to the road, their mother took a deep breath. "Well, as a salesperson, Wilma will tell me everything she thinks I want to hear. She'll point out every good thing about the house, but might not mention its flaws, or things that need work."

"Salespeople can be so slimy," Summer said, shaking her head and taking notes.

"You two will be my eyes, ears, and hands. When Wilma's telling me about the kitchen's ideal proximity to the living room, I want you opening cabinets, checking appliances, and testing the kitchen sink faucet. When she's going on and on about the spaciousness of the master bedroom, I want you inspecting the closet. When she's raving about the bathroom tile, I want you looking for mold. In every room, I want you checking the carpet for stains or pulls, ceiling for water damage, and windows for functionality."

"Wow." Maggie turned slightly in her seat to see Summer scribbling furiously.

"But most importantly, I want you to think about how the house feels, and whether you could picture yourself coming home there every day."

They drove for twenty minutes before turning onto a pretty, tree-lined street. As they followed the road to a small cul-de-sac, passing several big, new houses with lush green lawns and colorful gardens, kids riding bikes and families playing soccer and catch in front yards, Maggie found herself smiling. This neighborhood was completely different from their current one, where their closest neighbors were some very nice, but very quiet retirees, and you were likelier to see a Buick Le Sabre than a bike. Their current neighborhood also consisted of an odd assortment of dated houses in various states of disrepair and maintenance. Something was always going wrong in their own house—gutters collapsing in heavy rain, the back door getting stuck shut—and it usually took the landlord days to fix anything.

But the houses in this neighborhood were new, gorgeous, and needing only families to fill them.

"Whoa," Summer said when they stopped in front of a two-story, blue Colonial with a wraparound porch.

"Is this just a meeting spot?" Maggie tried to keep her hopes in check as she rolled down the window to smell the nearby rosebushes. "Was Wilma showing this house to other people?"

"Maybe I have the address wrong," their mother mumbled, pulling a piece of paper from her purse. "Nope. This is it."

Summer was out of the car before her mother had a chance to turn it off.

"Don't forget your gear." Maggie reached in the backseat for Summer's backpack.

"This is it."

Maggie and her mother climbed out of the car and stood on either side of Summer.

"We don't have to look anywhere else," Summer continued. Her eyes were wide, as though hypnotized by the delicate silver wind chime dangling from the porch roof. "We're home."

"I guess I'll hang on to this." Maggie removed the digital camera from Summer's backpack and slung the bag on one shoulder. She snapped a series of shots as she and her mother followed after Summer, who skipped down the red-brick path toward the porch and front door.

"You'll keep a level head, won't you, sweetie?" her mother asked, wringing her hands nervously. "And carefully evaluate everything I mentioned before forming a solid opinion?"

"You can count on me." Maggie might have been impressed, but unlike Summer, she could always prevent emotional reactions from interfering with logic. After all, this was just a house, with a few walls and maybe some fancy crown molding that served the same purpose as any other set of walls. Did it really matter where they lived, so long as where they lived kept out the rain and let in the sun?

It most certainly did, it turned out.

Maggie had been in nice houses before—never one of her own, of course, but Arnie's and Aimee's homes were both probably as large as this house, if not larger, and decorated with expensive-looking furniture and real artwork. Anytime she visited, she was always a tiny bit jealous on top of being happy to be there, and wondered what it was their parents knew that hers hadn't figured out—what they had that enabled their families to live in the same beautiful houses year after year, while her family rented one small place after the next.

But as nice as Arnie's and Aimee's houses were, they didn't compare to this one.

"Wilma, hello!" their mother sang, closing the front door behind and walking purposefully across the foyer to shake Wilma's hand.

Standing near the entrance with Summer, Maggie looked

around. It wasn't the impressive, wide staircase they stood near, or the large rooms that connected to the foyer. It wasn't the natural stone tile under their feet, or the shiny wooden floors that led to the rest of the house. It wasn't even the warm sunlight that streamed in through the room's many windows. And if anyone had asked what it was, really, the best Maggie could've come up with was that it just felt right—the air (cool and refreshing), the size (big, but not overwhelming), the way walking through that front door once felt like she'd done it a million times before.

"This *is* it," she whispered to Summer.

"Mom, may Maggie and I show ourselves around while you talk business?" Summer asked in her politest, most grown-up voice.

Since their mother and Wilma had barely gotten past the weather, let alone delved into business details, and since Maggie and Summer were supposed to be on flaw-finding duty, their mother looked at Summer, surprised. "Well, I suppose if Wilma says it's all right...."

"The bedrooms are upstairs," Wilma, an older, rather professorial-looking woman in a black suit and trendy tortoise-shell glasses, said with a smile.

Maggie and Summer exchanged quick, excited glances before dashing up the stairs. Their assigned task forgotten, they split up and hurried down the long hallway, popping in and out of four bedrooms, two bathrooms, and an office. The feeling Maggie felt stepping inside the house was only stronger upstairs, and nearly knocked her over when she reached the last bedroom on the right.

It wasn't the biggest bedroom (since her parents, being older and more than one person, got automatic dibs on the biggest), or even the second-biggest bedroom. But it was in the back of the house, which made it quieter than other rooms, and had two big windows on two walls, thanks to its corner location. The views from the windows looked like framed postcards; being on the cul-de-sac, the house was tucked away from all the others in the neighborhood, so instead of seeing into the neighbor's backyard or second-floor bathroom, she saw stretches of green field, trees and even a distant pond. Inside, the hardwood floors were warm, chocolate brown, and shiny, and the walls were painted her favorite shade of light blue—like the sky, but with a hint of lavender. But the best part, the very best part that made this room more hers than any other she'd ever stepped inside, was on the only wall that lacked windows or doors.

Bookshelves. Built right into the wall, and running its entire length.

Standing in the middle of the room, Maggie turned

slowly and pictured her favorite books neatly on display instead of crammed under her bed, in random drawers, or in her closet. She pictured a wide, white desk against one wall of windows, and herself sitting there, occasionally stopping to admire the view in between homework assignments. She pictured a full-size bed (instead of her current tiny twin-size), covered in soft white sheets, a blue-floral-print down comforter, and piles of pillows. She pictured the closet filled with new size-eight clothes and cute shoes. She kept picturing it until Summer burst through the door and stopped short.

"Maggie!" she gasped. "This is your room."

"I know," Maggie said, shaking her head at the odds.

"Let's go tell Mom."

Snapping back to their still-renting reality, Maggie hurried after Summer. She'd promised her mother a level head, and even if it had taken her all of ten seconds to break that promise, she could still pull it together for appearances while her mother kept her cool with Wilma.

She didn't have to try hard. Reaching the living room and finding Summer hovering impatiently near their mother and Wilma, Maggie gave her a quick shake of the head and patted the P.A. backpack to remind her that they still had a job to do. Once certain Summer could be trusted to keep quiet for a little while longer, Maggie turned her attention to the task at hand, dutifully followed the adults from one room to the next, and evaluated everything she was supposed to. She opened cabinets, tested faucets, took pictures, made notes, and came to a very important conclusion.

The house was perfect.

"So what do we think?" Wilma asked after they'd explored every last square inch and returned to the foyer.

"Can I say it *now*?" Summer whispered loudly to Maggie, hopping from one foot to the next.

"We're interested."

Maggie and Summer turned toward their mother, mouths wide in surprise.

"Aren't we?" Her expression was serious and business-like, but the twinkle in her eyes gave her away. She knew they'd already mentally arranged furniture and unpacked their bags.

"It's very nice," Maggie said, nodding and struggling to keep her voice level. Just because her mother knew didn't mean Wilma did—or should.

"When can we move in?" Summer asked, apparently not caring what Wilma knew.

"Why don't you two try out the front porch swing while we discuss details?"

Maggie would've preferred to never leave the house ever again—with enough research she could homeschool herself, after all—but she grabbed Summer's hand and hurried outside. The sooner details were discussed, the sooner they could move in.

"You saw me eat breakfast, right?"

Maggie sat next to Summer on the wide white porch swing.

"Rice Krispies with blueberries? Big glass of orange juice?"

Forcing herself to tear her attention away from the cluster of kids her age laughing and playing Frisbee in the cul-de-sac, Maggie looked at Summer curiously.

"I did wake up this morning, right? I took a shower, got dressed, ate breakfast, and drove to the most perfect house ever with you guys, right?"

"Did you spike your OJ with espresso?" Maggie asked, concerned. "You're starting to scare me."

"It just feels like a dream." Summer leaned against the back of the swing and looked across the front yard. "I know we're really here, but I can't believe we might actually get to *stay* here, someday."

"Me either," Maggie said, pressing her feet against the ground and gently rocking the swing. "But maybe it's just our time, you know? Just because we've never had anything like this before didn't necessarily mean we were never supposed to—even if it usually felt that way."

"So maybe this is our reward," Summer said thoughtfully.

"Our reward?"

"For getting through everything else. Dad losing his job, Mom and Dad fighting about money and bills, moving around . . . all of the hard stuff."

Maggie couldn't have said it better herself. Their family had stuck together and made it through some very tough times. They deserved something good—something *great*. And this house definitely qualified. "Just imagine Christmas morning," she said, leaning against Summer. "We'll get the biggest, tallest, fattest tree in the lot, just because we can."

"And pile hundreds of presents underneath, just because we can."

"And we'll get up really early, before the sun's even up, and come downstairs, and it'll be totally quiet, and totally dark except for the Christmas lights. And we'll take our stockings from the fireplace mantel, and wait for Mom and Dad to wake up."

"And it'll be snowing outside." Summer sighed happily.

"And it'll *definitely* be snowing outside. And later, after we've opened our hundreds of presents, we'll have a big breakfast with pancakes and hot chocolate and French toast. And then we'll stay in our pajamas, play with our toys, and watch movies all day."

Summer tilted her head up to look at Maggie. "It was worth it."

Before Maggie could agree, the front door opened and their mother stepped onto the porch. In the nanosecond it took for Maggie and Summer to leap from the swing, she'd cleared the steps and was halfway down the redbrick path that led to the driveway. "Mom?" Maggie called, taking Summer's hand again and hurrying from the porch.

"I was very clear."

Reaching the car, Maggie opened the back door for Summer, closed it after she'd climbed inside, and jumped in the passenger seat. Their mother already sat in the driver's seat, fumbling with her key chain.

"I couldn't have been clearer," she continued, unsuccessfully trying to shove one key after the next into the ignition. "Three bedrooms, one bathroom, living room, kitchen, move-in ready. That's it. That's all we need."

Maggie watched her nervously. "Mom, it's the one with the black rubber—"

"But instead she shows us this—this *monstrosity*. Five bedrooms, four bathrooms, living room, dining room, kitchen, den, wine cellar, two fireplaces, fancy appliances, central air-conditioning. I mean, who does she think we are? Did I introduce myself as Mrs. Hilton? I don't think so."

Leaning across the console, Maggie grabbed both her mother's trembling hands with one hand, and the key chain with the other.

"Thank you," her mother said softly when Maggie gently placed the right key in the ignition. Sighing, she leaned her head back and closed her eyes. "I don't know if I can do this."

"Do what?" Maggie asked. "What happened?"

"I can't disappoint you girls." Turning slightly in the seat, she blew Summer a kiss and then gave Maggie a small, sad smile.

"We're not disappointed," Maggie promised, even though she had no idea why her mother thought they might be.

"You love this house. Your faces lit up like the sun the second you stepped inside. And all I want is for your faces to do that every single day."

Knowing she had to keep a calm, steady expression but fearing what she knew was coming, Maggie focused on the small freckle just under her mother's right eye.

"This isn't it," she finally said sadly. "And I'm so, so sorry.

If there was any way we could swing it, we would, but it's just not in our price range. It's not even close. If we never took another vacation or bought new furniture—or even food and clothing, for that matter—it still wouldn't be in our price range."

"So why did she show it to us?" Summer asked quietly from the backseat.

"Because she's evil," Maggie said simply.

"She's not evil. She's a salesperson. She knew this was too much, but thought that if we just saw it we'd fall so in love, we might sell your firstborn children to pay for it."

"Ew." Summer cringed.

"Exactly," Maggie agreed.

"Yes, but I should've known better. I mean, I *did* know better, but I just got caught up in the moment. I lost my head." She frowned. "I'm sorry, girls. You know your father and I just want to make you happy."

"We're happy!" Maggie said brightly, forcing a smile. "So this isn't it. There are tons of houses out there, and we won't stop looking until we find the one that's meant for us."

"Absolutely." Apparently wanting to prove it was no big deal, Summer unzipped her backpack and pulled out a notebook and pen to prepare for the next evaluation.

As her mother started the car and pulled away from the

curb, Maggie slid down in her seat and watched the blue Colonial grow smaller. She wanted to be as unaffected as her little sister appeared to be, but couldn't help but feel disappointed. Maybe they just weren't meant to have a nice house; maybe they were always meant to have less than everyone else seemed to have. Or, maybe they really hadn't earned it yet. And if that was the case, she didn't know if they ever would, because she couldn't imagine what else they'd have to go through before they did.

9. "Maggie Bean." Smirking, Erin tilted her head down to peer over the top of her sunglasses. "Nice of you to join us."

"Sorry," Maggie said, jogging across the sand. "My mom got wrapped up in something this morning and—"

"Doesn't matter, you're here just in time."

"Oh." Reaching the lifeguard stand, Maggie smiled. She'd been dreading Erin's reprimand for forty-five whole minutes—while her mother finished e-mailing Wilma, while Summer scrambled for socks without holes *after* her mother finished e-mailing Wilma, during the drive to camp, and as she sprinted the final distance across the endless lawn to the beach. She was only ten minutes late, but on the first day of her second week at Camp Sound View, that was about twenty minutes too many. "Thanks."

"The pump broke, and my lips are chapped."

When Erin turned her attention back to her clipboard without further explanation, Maggie scanned the area surrounding the lifeguard stand. "Inner tubes?"

"And rafts. Ten of each. They'll be pretty hard to inflate since they're brand-new and have never been inflated before, so you'll want to get started right away."

"These are huge." Maggie shuffled across the sand and used both hands to lift one gigantic, flattened inner tube from the stack. "I only have two lungs."

"Which apparently work very well, given your performance last week."

"But the first groups will be here any minute."

Hugging the clipboard to her chest, Erin faced Maggie. "Your concern is sweet. But we have everything under control."

"But—" Before Maggie could protest, Erin spun around and marched toward Polly, the swim instructor with the short blond bob who lounged on the sand a few feet away and yawned like she'd just woken up. Maggie waited for Erin to scold Polly for still being half-asleep while on duty, or blast the whistle in her ear to jar her to consciousness, but all she did was squat, talk quietly, and giggle.

Maggie sank to the sand. It wasn't worth an argument,

even though Erin had said last week that Maggie would be helping Polly with groups of campers this week. The first few days had been introductory free-for-alls, for Maggie as well as the campers, and swim time had been devoted to water games and icebreakers instead of instruction. The lessons were supposed to start today, and though she'd been looking forward to serving an actual purpose and getting to know the kids, she wasn't about to put up a fight. If Erin assigned Maggie inner-tube-and-raft-inflation duty to keep her out of the water, there was no telling what she'd do if somehow forced to do anything else against her will. What would be Maggie's next task then? Collecting the thousands of rocks scattered across the beach and buffering their sharp edges in the interest of camper safety? Building a life-size sand castle with actual rooms for campers to hang out in during bad weather?

Sighing, she dragged the gigantic flattened inner tube across her lap and opened the small plastic air valve. She would do as she was asked, just like she always did. If they really were in a bind and needed her help, which was why Adam had hired her in a hurry in the first place, then she'd just have to hope that that became apparent very quickly, and that she was put to real use out of necessity.

"Good morning, my little angels!"

Blowing into the air valve, Maggie raised her eyes to see

Erin jump up and open her arms, as if to embrace all of the dozens of campers descending onto the beach at the same time.

"I hope you're ready for a great day of learning and fun!"

Maggie watched Polly stand and stretch, and Ben and Jason (the other male swim instructor) jog out of the water and head for their groups. She'd learned last week that the boys got to work extra early every day for a morning workout of alternating laps and beach sprints, and had been happy to spot them in the water when she finally reached the beach earlier. Swearing off boys entirely didn't make being embarrassed in front of them any easier.

As campers divided into their swim groups and dashed toward the water, Maggie focused on breathing—a suddenly laborious task. The inner tubes were made of thick black rubber, and even though she inhaled and exhaled until her lungs threatened to pop or shrivel into nothing, the rubber hardly moved.

"Mags!"

Maggie squeezed the air valve shut with two fingers to free her mouth so she could lift her head. Her lips were already dry, but she managed to smile as Aimee sprinted toward her.

"What're you doing?" Aimee asked, gently kicking the stack of rubber with her sneaker.

"Teaching campers what to do when they need a flotation device because they never learned how to swim."

"Why aren't you in the water?"

"Tell you later," Maggie said, spotting Erin talking to a counselor near the lifeguard stand. "How's your morning?"

"Fantastic. Had a great early meeting with the girls—"

"The girls?"

"Tillie, Morgan, Sonia, and the rest of the Figure Eights."

"This place has an ice-skating rink? In the middle of summer?"

"Maybe you should lay off the oxygen," Aimee teased. "Figure Eights is our group name. We have one every year. Last year, when we were going into seventh grade, we were Seventh Heaven. The year before that, we were the Unstoppable Sixes. The year before *that*—"

"I get it," Maggie said, keeping one eye on Erin. After being late, she didn't need to get in trouble for socializing on the job. "What was your meeting about?"

"We have one every day. They're basically to talk about our nights, and plan our day together."

"Doesn't every group get a schedule that they follow the entire summer?"

Tricia Rayburn

"Yes, but what happens within each hour of that schedule changes every day."

"Oh."

"Anyway, we also meet to select the Queen of the Day. We found out Tillie had a fight with her boyfriend last night, so we chose her to reign all day today, and receive eight hours of compliments and positive energy." Aimee turned slightly to wave at her group. "Great bathing suit, Tils!"

"Huh."

"Anyway, I have to get back. But you'll tell me later why you're sitting by yourself and blowing up water toys?"

"If my brain cells are still functioning after severe oxygen deprivation, you bet."

"Great. See you later!"

Maggie watched her best friend run away and join an entire circle of best friends. They may have been seasonal best friends, but Aimee had been attending Camp Sound View since kindergarten, which meant she had seven seasons of jokes, gossip, and history with them. Maggie knew this happened every summer, but this was the first time she'd actually witnessed it in person. And she wouldn't have said so out loud, but it actually stung a little.

The small stinging worsened as Aimee ran into the water with her group and as the other campers began their lessons with Erin, Polly, Jason, and Ben. Shifting so that her back was to the water, Maggie forced another breath into the tube, and thought about Peter. For the first time since their disastrous conversation, she found herself getting mad at him instead of sad at his not wanting to be with her. If Peter hadn't rejected her, she would've been too busy going to the movies, miniature golfing, sunning at the beach, or partaking in hundreds of other new-couple activities to spend one sad second on the couch watching daytime television. And if she hadn't been spending *hundreds* of sad seconds on the couch watching daytime television, her mother never would've decided that she was bored or unmotivated enough to be suckered into a summer job. And if she hadn't been suckered into a summer job, she never would've seen her best friend with other best friends, been stuck blowing air into tubes, and wishing she were home watching daytime television.

Peter Applewood had turned her into a wannabe couch potato.

The thought was so distressing, she started firing shorter, faster breaths into the tube. How dare he do that? Who did he think he was? So what if he was the star shortstop on the school baseball team? So what if half the girls in their class watched his every move and whispered to one another behind their hands whenever he was near? Did that really give him the right to—

"Anthony!"

Maggie's breath caught in her throat when Erin's voice shot across the beach.

"Get back here *right now!*"

Swiveling to face the water and standing on her knees to get a better view, Maggie saw a young boy splashing near the far end of the roped-off swimming area. He was by himself, and about twenty feet from the closest group of campers.

"Do you think this is funny?" Erin shrieked. "Because I'm not laughing. *No one's* laughing, Anthony!"

Maggie didn't mean to laugh right when Erin so adamantly insisted no one was, but the chuckle escaped her dry lips before she could stop it. The boy obviously knew how to swim (especially since he smirked toward shore every time he came up from underwater), and was just trying to get the exact reaction Erin was giving him.

"I don't care how you act when you're with your counselor, but when you're with *me*, you will listen to *me!*"

"I'm guessing she didn't share her toys as a little girl."

Squinting against the sun, Maggie looked up to see Ben standing next to her.

"Why is she so mad?" Maggie glanced back at the water. "He's okay, isn't he?"

"Of course he is." Grinning, he crouched next to her. "I'll let you in on a little Camp Sound View secret."

Maggie held her breath. He was so close, she could see individual water droplets on his face.

"Erin is many things," he said quietly, still grinning. "She's smart, cute, organized, punctual, and very committed to her job. But I've known her a long time, and the one thing she is not—never has been and never will be—is kid-friendly."

"That would seem like a detriment to the job she's so committed to."

"With Erin, it's about the power, not the kids. They freak her out. And what's worse is that they know they freak her out."

"Anthony Luciano, you have *ten seconds* to get back here or I'm coming in after you!"

"And she really thinks the ear-numbing screams work?"

"Apparently," he said, shaking his head. "See how they all keep swimming, talking, and laughing? You and I are the only ones paying attention to her right now. She refuses to accept that there's really only one thing you have to remember when dealing with kids."

"And what's that?" Maggie asked, turning to look at him.

"That they're just miniature versions of us."

"And we definitely don't respond well to shrieking demands."

"If she were coming at me like that, I'd bolt in the other direction, not hang around to see what else she had to say."

Maggie was about to comment on how such a simple concept seemed to make a ton of sense, when cool drops of water fell across her shoulders. Turning around, she found a group of soaking wet boys standing behind her.

"Maggie, meet the Freshwater Phantoms, seven of the most amazing fifth graders to ever take to the high seas."

"Hi, guys," Maggie said, smiling at the boys.

Ben stood from his crouched position and faced his campers. "Are you ready for your very important assignment?"

The boys nodded somberly.

"Great. Now, as you can see, Maggie is just one person—a very strong person, but still, just one person. She's been asked to blow up all of these tubes and rafts, but with just one person on the job, that could take all summer. Plus, these tubes and rafts are for all of us to enjoy."

Maggie looked at the boys. Fifth graders might've been miniature versions of themselves, but they could still be impatient and rambunctious; these kids stood still and listened to

Ben as though he was some sort of little-boy God addressing them in an empty room, and not on a beach surrounded by a million distractions.

"Guys, Maggie—and all of Camp Sound View, for that matter—needs our help. Are you up to the challenge?"

"What?" She'd been so busy appreciating his calm, effective approach, it hadn't occurred to her what he was actually doing. "Ben, that's not necessary. I—"

"We're ready!" a curly haired Freshwater Phantom declared for the group.

"Good."

Maggie was about to attempt another protest, but stopped when she noticed Ben trying not to smile.

"Start with the rafts. And take your time. If you need to rest, rest. This isn't a contest, and we're not trying to break any records."

With one nod from Ben, the boys were off. Maggie thought they might revert to rambunctious, impatient fifth graders as they scrambled for rafts, but once they each had one, they simply found empty spots in the sand and began blowing.

"Ben, this is great, thank you," Maggie said as he sat next to her. "But shouldn't you guys be in the water? I don't want Erin to scream at you, too."

"She won't," he said, dragging a flattened inner tube from the stack. "And if she does, I'll just remind her that I'm building camper relationships. These guys need to trust and respect me if they're going to learn anything. I've asked them for help, they feel important, and tomorrow we can really focus on our lessons with mutual trust already established."

"Okay," Maggie said doubtfully as Erin blew three long whistles at another swimming camper gone astray.

"Besides, fifth graders are full of hot air."

Maggie laughed and pulled the inner tube she'd been working on pre-Erin-freak-out back in her lap. With Ben next to her and the Freshwater Phantoms behind her, the only trouble she had blowing into the tube now was keeping air from escaping as she smiled around the small plastic air valve.

10. Maggie stood on the front porch of Arnie's MudPuddle lake house, finger poised just above the doorbell. She spent so much time at Arnie's lake house, she usually just let herself in and announced her arrival by yelling for Arnie once inside, but this was her first time back since the Peter Applewood disaster. It felt different now—like the house itself, and not just Peter, had rejected her.

"Central-air allergy acting up again?"

Maggie stumbled backward as the front door flew open. "I didn't ring," she huffed.

"You never ring. And you've been standing like a statue in the sweltering heat for eight minutes and thirty-seven seconds."

"It's not that hot," Maggie said, wiping her damp forehead.

"I'd rather not hold this debate outside since my brain tends to swell to nonfunctioning proportions in 120 percent humidity."

"Fine." Taking what she hoped was an unnoticeable deep breath, Maggie brushed past Arnie through the door.

"Better?" he asked with a grin, closing the door behind them.

"Getting there," she said wearily, eyeing the couch she and Peter had shared during *Shrek* marathons, the Nintendo Wii Arnie and Peter were usually glued to, and the fireplace she and Peter had sat in front of the first time they'd hung out in Arnie's house together. Not all of the memories were perfect—they'd sat in front of the fireplace together after he'd found her passed out on the dock and brought her inside last fall, a truly mortifying moment from which she was still recovering—but they were still nice enough to make her heart sink while standing in the living room. "Where are you going?"

Arnie froze in the kitchen doorway. "To get snacks?"

"I'm not hungry," Maggie insisted, heart racing. Standing in the living room was one thing, but going into the kitchen would be like revisiting the scene of a very bad accident— she'd look around in disbelief, picture the way everything went down, and wish she could turn back time to prevent it from happening. "Or thirsty."

"But I'm starving. And watching you stand in that heat made me rather parched."

"Are we working in your room?"

"Both parental units are on the premises, so, yes."

"I'll meet you there."

Maggie knew Arnie watched her curiously as she bolted from the living room—given that he was not only a boy but also Peter's cousin, she hadn't told him about the embarrassing incident that caused her current strange behavior. But she kept her head lowered and hurried down the hallway, up the stairs, and into the second bedroom on the right. Since this was Arnie's family's summer house, his room lacked the same amenities—a forty-two-inch plasma-screen TV, an extensive DVD library that Netflix would envy, and a stocked Red Bull cooler—as his regular bedroom in their permanent home. This room still had a twenty-six-inch plasma-screen TV, smaller collection of DVDs, and a refrigerator big enough to fit two Red Bull four-packs, but it didn't compare to the living room or kitchen, so they didn't hang out there much. In fact, once inside, her heart slowed to a steady thumping, her stomach stopped turning, and she couldn't picture Peter there at all. Which meant they'd never been in the room at the same time, which meant it was completely safe.

"Okay," Arnie said, coming into the room and pushing the door closed with one foot, "I know you're not hungry or thirsty, but I have pretzels, strawberries, sugar-free chocolate pudding, granola, and Soy Crisps. And bottled water and unsweetened iced tea."

"Are we expecting company?"

"You know I like choices." Leaning over the bed, Arnie opened his arms and lifted his chin to unload enough food to feed everyone at Pound Patrollers.

"What's with the bags?" Maggie took a plastic Baggie of pretzel nuggets from the pile.

"Portion control," Arnie explained, taking another plastic Baggie of sliced strawberries. "Anyway, we have a lot of work to do, so I thought we should have a lot of fuel."

"Don't several single-portion-size snacks kind of defeat the purpose of portion control?"

Already done with the strawberries, Arnie pouted and tossed the Baggie of Soy Crisps he'd just picked up back on the pile. "Let's get started."

The one thing Arnie never went without, whether he was at his primary home, his summer home, or traveling somewhere in-between, was his beloved seventeen-inch MacBook Pro. Some kids had favorite stuffed animals or blankies they clung to for comfort; instead of a ratty teddy bear or worn knit throw, Arnie clung to his MacBook Pro. Maggie followed him now to his big black desk, where the silver laptop was up and running and playing some kind of dance music. Surrounding the laptop were notebooks, pens, Post-its, highlighters, and stacks of paper.

"You've been busy," Maggie said. "I'm impressed."

Arnie pulled an overstuffed armchair from the corner of the room to the desk and motioned for Maggie to sit.

"So how scary was Electra last week?"

"Dude," he said, his fingers flying across the keyboard as he plopped in the wooden desk chair. "That was a whole new level of crazy. Which makes what we're doing today even more important."

"What *are* we doing today?" Maggie leaned forward to see the laptop screen.

"Choosing the general template and discussing the beginning content of the Patrol This website." Arnie punched the return key, watched the screen fill with several boxes, and turned the laptop toward Maggie. "These are their template suggestions."

Maggie examined the four website pages lined next to one another. The first featured photos of a group of smiling, generic-looking kids as they played soccer, jogged on a woodsy trail, and ate orange slices. The second showed an animated lion in a PATROL THIS vest and badge monitoring the eating habits of other jungle animals, including a trio of banana-munching monkeys. The third displayed a bright red stop sign with PATROL THIS and CHANGE YOUR LIFE in big black letters, and five examples of how—the first being a longer life. She didn't think it could get any worse than that—the glaring warning that you might die without help—but the fourth template was, without question, the very worst of all.

"You've got to be kidding me."

Arnie looked at her, then back at the screen. "I know they're not especially innovative or original, but—"

"How'd they get that picture?" Maggie grabbed one corner of the laptop and pulled it closer. "I look like a walrus!"

"You do not look like a walrus."

The fourth website template was totally blank—white background, no text—except for the enormous shot of her and Arnie wearing PATROL THIS T-shirts and standing with their arms across each other's shoulders. "Darn that Aunt Violetta," she grumbled, recalling her aunt's insistence to take their picture at the last Pound Patrollers meeting. She'd said she wanted it for her scrapbook, but had Maggie known her scrapbook was going to be online and available for millions of people all over the world to see, she might've brushed her hair first. "And I do look like a walrus. My face is huge, my forehead's shiny, and I look like I never lost a pound in that baggy T-shirt."

"Maggie," Arnie said, looking at the picture and shaking his head, "you're beautiful."

Her mouth already hung open in surprise at seeing herself on the screen, so immediate protest could've—and should've—flown out quickly and easily. But Arnie's compliment actually forced her mouth shut and left her temporarily speechless. The only people who'd ever told her she was beautiful were her mother and Aimee, and the words sounded very different coming from someone besides her mother and best friend. And even if Arnie was just being nice because he was her friend, or because he looked great in the same photo and wanted to keep it on the website, he was still a boy.

A boy who didn't think she looked like a walrus. A boy who thought she was beautiful.

"Of course," he said when her uncharacteristic silence grew louder than the music still pulsating from the laptop, "my hair was falling especially well that day, and purple is perfect for my skin tone, so the picture was bound to be a winner."

"Of course," Maggie agreed. He focused on the screen, so she did too, but out of the corners of her eyes, she noticed his face was redder than normal.

"Arnold Bartholomew Gunderson."

Maggie didn't know whether to be relieved for the distraction or scared for their safety when Arnie's mother threw open the bedroom door. She stood in the doorway, wearing designer exercise clothes (black leggings, a sleeveless black top, and futuristic-looking silver sneakers), an iPod, and a BlackBerry. Her dark brown hair was twisted tightly on top of her head. She had to be around Maggie's mother's age, but looked more like a college student.

"Holy cow," Arnie muttered under his breath before closing the laptop and swiveling in his chair. "Yes, Mom?" he asked politely, his voice back to regular volume.

"I was just enjoying a nice leisurely afternoon of watching C-SPAN, reading *The Wall Street Journal*, and e-mailing clients while doing my stress-reducing ten-mile run on the treadmill, when a ton of reminders popped up and interrupted my good time." Standing in the doorway, she started reading from her BlackBerry. "Arnie practice flute, Arnie swim in lake, Arnie jog around lake, Arnie read one hundred pages of book of his choice. Nowhere does it say anything about Arnie hiding in his room and playing on his computer all day. Hello, Maggie."

"Hello, Mrs. Gunderson."

"Have you done any of these things today? How many

times do we have to talk about summer vacation not being an excuse for lazing about and letting your mind and body atrophy, but being an opportunity to enlighten yourself and grow as an individual?" Suddenly distracted, she looked at the bed. "Please don't tell me you plan to eat all of that."

"Mom, it's only four o'clock. I have time."

"Time's an illusion. You think the day's long, and before you know it, you're ready to collapse into bed with a migraine, but you still have to answer seventy-five e-mails and return twenty-one calls."

Arnie shifted his eyes toward Maggie without turning his head, and Maggie fought the urge to throw her arms around him in a protective, reassuring hug. She'd only met Mrs. Gunderson a few times—mostly because her job as a corporate lawyer kept her very busy and traveling a lot, and also because Arnie did his best to avoid her whenever she *was* around—and each meeting was even more intimidating than the one before.

"Answer me, please. Some of us have to work."

"I'll swim when Maggie leaves, practice the flute after that, jog around the lake after dinner, and read one hundred pages before bed."

"Of what?"

Arnie looked at his mother.

"One hundred pages of what?"

"*The Sun Also Rises,*" Arnie said without batting an eye.

"I'd like a five p.m. update."

"You got it," Arnie said, saluting as his mother answered her ringing BlackBerry and dashed from the doorway.

"Hemingway?" Maggie raised her eyebrows.

"Thought I'd see what the fuss is about."

Amazed, Maggie watched him pull a copy from the side pocket of his cargo shorts and toss it on the desk. "I guess I have a lot to do today. We should probably get back to work."

Maggie frowned as Arnie opened the laptop and pulled up the website templates. He joked about his parents a lot, and called the family housekeeper "Mom" and driver "Dad" since he saw them more and thought they knew him better than his actual mom and dad, but it was clear their absence and infrequent, uncomfortable presence bothered him more than he'd like to admit. Even now, he sat up extra straight in his chair, tapped one foot, and nibbled his lip while staring at the laptop screen. "Are you okay?"

"I think we should go with the fourth one," Arnie said, as if he hadn't heard her.

Maggie waited to see if he'd change his mind about avoiding her question. When he stared silently at the computer without blinking, she forced her attention back to the website templates. "Okay . . . but there's not much going on there. Besides your good hair, I mean."

"Exactly. It's an empty slate. We can come up with a ton of our own ideas and see what the company thinks."

"That sounds fun, but time-consuming."

"It won't be that bad. And after seeing the first three ridiculously cheesy options, do we really have a choice? Especially if our names and faces are attached?"

Looking at the diet-enforcing lion, Maggie nodded. He had a point. No sane kid was going to want to surf a site that made him or her feel silly for doing so. "Do we have to use that picture?"

He looked at her and grinned. "Of course not. We can hold a professional photo shoot to get the very best options, if you want."

She didn't love the idea of being on the Internet for everyone all over the world to see, but she did think it was important that they do this right. The goal was to reach kids and inspire them to make better decisions that would help them lead happier lives. For that to happen, the kids needed to first feel like they hadn't done anything wrong, and that they weren't alone. And what better way was there to convince them of that than other kids who'd been there and understood what they were going through, rather than parents, teachers, or anyone else who hadn't?

"Okay," she said finally. "But if we're going to do it, we're going to really do it."

"Absolutely."

"Like, if we're doing pictures, we should probably have before-and-after shots of ourselves."

"Let's not go crazy."

"I'm serious. Kids need to trust us and know we're not frauds."

Thinking it over, Arnie nodded slowly. "And maybe we could write short accounts of what we went through."

"And what we still go through."

"In our own voices."

"Exactly."

He looked at her. "This just might work."

As he closed the other website templates and started scribbling notes, Maggie hoped he was right. After being hurt by Peter, shunned by Erin, and misled by Wilma, she could use the positive distraction. And after witnessing the painful exchange between Arnie and his mother, she knew he could use some of the same.

They might have been weight-loss-success stories, but they were still works-in-progress. And right then, they needed chubby kids everywhere as much as chubby kids everywhere needed them.

11. "Did you crash on the beach last night?"

"It's seven thirty already?" Maggie dropped the stack of life preservers she carried to check her watch. "How is it seven thirty already?"

"No tent, no bonfire, no sleeping bag," Ben said, looking around as he neared Maggie. "You're either a hardcore camper, or working serious overtime."

"Sorry, I thought I'd be done by the time you got here for your workout." She offered a small smile as she knelt down to gather the life preservers.

"No apologies necessary. It's a big beach, and I'm happy to share." Dropping his backpack and towel to the sand, he crouched down to help Maggie. "But please don't tell me Erin asked you to come in this early."

"She didn't."

"Good. That would've been low, even for her."

Carefully balancing a tower of orange foam in her arms, Maggie stood slowly and shuffled toward the lifeguard stand.

"So what are you doing here?"

Maggie deposited the stack next to three others and brushed sand from her hands. "I'm trying to get my job back."

"She *fired* you? Are you kidding me?" Ben added the last stack to the neat line of life preservers and looked at her in disbelief. "Did you talk to Adam? Because I'll find him right now and tell him—"

"She didn't fire me," Maggie said, reassured, touched— and surprised—by his apparent concern. "But she might as well have, for all the time I've spent in the water. Last night I made a list of every little ridiculous thing she could ever ask me to do so that I could come here early and finish each one."

"Wow," Ben said, grinning appreciatively. "So what time did you get here?"

"Six." Her dad had balked when she'd asked him to drop her off on the way to work, especially since the sky was still dusky gray with night, but agreed after she promised him the rest of the swim instructors awaited her at the beach for early CPR training.

"I bet the sunrise was awesome."

"It was, actually." She smiled. If she'd ever been awake early enough to see the sun rise, she'd certainly never been outside. And she hadn't even thought about it that morning until she was already on the beach, cleaning goggles—she'd held up a pair to inspect their clarity and suddenly noticed the sky turning shades of pink and lavender.

"Do you need any help finishing up?"

"Oh no, that's okay. I—"

"Dude!"

Maggie and Ben spun around to see Jason hobbling across the sand.

"I don't think I have it in me today."

Ben shook his head. "I knew you were never going to get out of there."

As Jason groaned and collapsed in the sand, Maggie resumed straightening the stacks of life preservers. She wanted to ask if he was okay, considering all the noise he was making and the fact that he was bundled up in baggy gray sweatpants, a navy hooded sweatshirt, and flip-flops with socks—it had been eighty degrees and humid when she left the house almost two hours earlier—but she still felt like a guest who'd shown up too early to the party. She thought it was better to pretend she wasn't there.

"It was *American Idol* karaoke." Flopping on his back, Jason covered his face with his baseball hat. "I finally made it to the finals. I couldn't just leave."

"How long did it take you to get to the finals?"

"*Four hours.* Plus about twenty more before last night."

"Did you win?"

Jason rolled on his side and brought his knees to his chest. "No," he said, pouting. "I did Whitney."

Maggie smiled when Ben cracked up.

"Hey, at least I take a risk! Not like other people who sing the same simple Billy Joel song every single time."

"I make no apologies," Ben said, still laughing. "'Piano Man' is a perpetual crowd-pleaser."

"Whatever. At least I saved every other sixteen-year-old guy in the room from having to learn a very important lesson the hard way."

"'Cause I'm sure every other sixteen-year-old in the room couldn't wait to attempt Whitney Houston."

Maggie giggled. So much for being invisible.

"Anyway, between the emotional roller coaster, lack of sleep, and vat of buttered popcorn I consumed, that water's not looking especially inviting right now."

"Suit yourself."

As Jason rolled onto his other side, away from them, Ben turned back to Maggie.

"*American Idol* karaoke?" she teased.

"It's a very addictive video game."

"With a microphone!" Jason called without turning over.

"Are you any good?"

"Not at all. Which is why 'Piano Man' is my song of choice. The game has only one other song with a simpler melody, but singing Kelly Clarkson just crosses a line."

"Sounds fun."

"If you like humiliating yourself in front of groups of people, it definitely is." Glancing over his shoulder, he shook his head in mock disappointment. "But there is such a thing as taking it too seriously."

Since Maggie had talked to Jason the least out of all the swim instructors and didn't know him well enough to poke friendly fun, she started wiping down the lifeguard stand.

"Are you sure you don't need any help?"

"I'm sure, thanks." She smiled. He sounded concerned again.

"Then I should probably start swimming. One of us has to be awake for the kids today," he said, louder.

When Jason waved one hand without looking up, Ben smiled once more at Maggie and headed for the water. He placed his backpack, T-shirt, and sneakers in a neat pile on the beach, dove in the water, and started doing brisk laps.

She didn't know if it was because she appreciated his natural athleticism, early morning exercise commitment, friendliness toward her, or a combination of all three, but for some reason, watching Ben swim reminded her of watching Peter play baseball. She'd gone to countless games with Arnie and cheered in the stands every time Peter hit, caught, or even dropped the ball. It didn't matter if the team won or lost, or if Peter had anything to do with either outcome—she just loved being there to support him.

She'd been his biggest fan, and even though he'd come with Arnie to several of her swim meets, he certainly hadn't been hers. She wasn't about to make the same mistake twice.

So, while Ben swam and Jason slept, Maggie pretended they weren't there, and continued wiping down the lifeguard stand. When not one droplet of lake water residue remained, she crawled between the chair's wooden legs and scrubbed underneath. She wiped, scrubbed, and polished until the stand shone like new, and then she shoved the dirty towels into her backpack so Erin couldn't complain about the leftover mess. When that was done, she scoured the beach for litter and random artifacts that had washed ashore. There wasn't much—after twenty minutes she'd only found an empty juice box and an unidentifiable green piece of plastic—but she walked a half mile in either direction, just in case. Once satisfied the beach was clear, she returned to the lifeguard stand and started rewrapping balls of gauze.

"What is this?"

Maggie turned around to see Erin standing just outside the trail entrance, one hand on her hip, the other holding a walkie-talkie in the air as though poised for self-defense.

"This is me recovering," Jason moaned without moving. "I'll be fine in ten minutes. Maybe twenty. Thirty, tops."

"I stopped hoping for your recovery a long time ago," Erin said, not bothering to look at Jason as she marched across the stand.

"Ouch." Rolling onto his back, Jason brought one hand to his chest to cover his wounded heart.

"What is this?" Erin fired the question at Maggie like she'd done something wrong. "Why are you here already?"

Maggie had tried to prepare herself for Erin's unhappy surprise, but her face reddened, anyway. "I'm working," she said softly, her voice cracking. "I'm *working*," she said again, firmly.

"No one asked you to get to work early. And you shouldn't be here unsupervised. I'm sure Adam would be thrilled to know you're wandering the beach alone and opening the door to camp liability and lawsuits. Maybe I should—"

"Give it a rest, Erin."

Maggie really didn't want to be relieved when Ben joined them, apparently done with the last leg of his beach sprints, but she felt her face cool immediately. He seemed to have some soothing effect on Erin, and Maggie wasn't too proud to be grateful.

"She wasn't alone. You know Jason and I are here every morning."

"He's hardly here." Erin folded her arms over her chest.

"I just wanted to get everything done early so I could help when the campers arrived," Maggie said boldly.

"Really." Erin smirked slightly, as though this was a game she'd already won. "First aid kits?"

"Restocked and reorganized according to most-used products—Band-Aids, gauze, medical tape, rubbing alcohol—"

"Life preservers?"

"Cleaned, straps tested and stacked by size."

"Water cooler?"

"Refilled."

"Goggles?"

"Spotless."

"Snorkels?

"Unclogged."

"Balls?"

"Inflated."

Erin paused. Frowning, she circled the lifeguard stand.

"I also patched holes in the inner tubes and rafts, cleaned the lifeguard stand, picked up litter, folded towels, laminated a weekly weather forecast for your clipboard, trimmed bushes lining the trail that leads to the beach, and raked the sand in the most-well-traveled spots to remove any especially large rocks or sticks."

After carefully examining Maggie's work, Erin stopped circling and looked at her. "Why?"

Maggie opened her mouth. That was one question she hadn't anticipated, and telling Erin that she was tired of being treated like a servant would be admitting that Erin had gotten under her skin. Maggie didn't want to give her the satisfaction. "I was hired to be a junior swim instructor," she finally said.

"How're the vocal chords this morning, Whitney?"

Polly had arrived and crouched near Jason, who still lay in a sad lump.

"Your fault," he grumbled as she patted his back. "All your fault."

"You'll work with Jason today," Erin said firmly, as though she'd made the decision out of practical necessity and not because Maggie had beaten her to the daily punch. "The campers will be here any second, so go talk to him, see if he can stand, and come up with a plan."

"Great," Maggie said happily, trying to prevent her smile from taking over her face. "Thank you."

When Erin turned away and started making notes on her clipboard without answering, Maggie snapped shut the first aid kit she'd been working on and headed for Jason.

"That was awesome," Ben whispered, walking with her.

"You know what this place needs?" Jason mumbled as they neared. "A cabana. With lounge chairs, refreshing drinks, snacks, and maybe a nice flat-screen."

"No more microphone for him." Polly stood and brushed her sandy hands on her shorts.

"I didn't bring drinks, snacks, or a flat-screen, but I'll help you any other way I can today," Maggie said, suddenly slightly nervous. Just because Erin had assigned her to Jason's group didn't mean Jason would be happy about it.

"My angel." Jason lifted his head from the sand slowly, as if it weighed fifty pounds, and looked at her. "Someday, when hitting the high notes in 'I Will Always Love You' is as easy as tying my shoes, I'll sing it for you to express my deep gratitude."

"How about Saturday?" Polly nudged him with her toe.

"As in four days from now?"

"Same time, same place." Polly smiled at Maggie. "You should come too. All of the counselors will be there."

"Really?" Maggie sighed on the inside. Couldn't she have just said she'd think about it instead of sounding so surprised?

"Well, almost everyone," she said, lowering her voice and tilting her head toward Erin.

"It'll be fun," Ben said. "Just don't steal my thunder by outdoing me on 'Piano Man.'" He grinned.

"Okay," Maggie said without even processing whether she already had plans (probably not) or related logistics (parental permission).

"Sorry to break it up," Erin called, "but the campers are on their way. Let's try to look like we care."

As Ben and Polly each grabbed one of Jason's hands and pulled him from the sand, Maggie returned to the lifeguard stand. Taking off her T-shirt, shorts, and flip-flops and placing them on top of her backpack, she replayed the conversation that had just taken place. She'd just been invited to a party. A *real* party, with older kids. She'd gone to tons of birthday parties for kids at school over the years, but she'd never been to a party that didn't involve cake, ice cream, and piles of presents.

The invitation raised a lot of questions (how she'd get to Polly's, what she'd wear, who she'd talk to once there), but she was certain of two things: This never would've happened a year ago, and she couldn't wait to tell Aimee.

12. "Is this another one of Wilma's sneaky sales tactics?" Maggie asked, standing between her mother and a flat tractor tire that had apparently been too heavy to throw out, so was just left in the middle of the patchy front lawn and filled with gray rocks. "So we get desperate and love whatever she shows us next, no matter the price tag?"

"I'm afraid not." Her mother opened a manila folder and flipped through a stack of printed papers. "I searched the online listings myself and told her which ones we wanted to look at."

"Did you like this one because we wouldn't have to buy as much furniture to fill it?" Summer stepped carefully on a tall stack of yellowing newspapers and took a picture of the small, sagging, carnation-pink house.

"Didn't anyone ever teach you girls not to judge a book by its cover?" Aimee asked from the edge of the yard, where she surveyed the front of the house from top to bottom.

"Yes," Maggie said automatically.

"You'd be amazed at what a fresh coat of paint and some simple landscaping can do to a shabby exterior. And who knows what's on the other side of that front door?"

"A big black hole, from the looks of it," Maggie's mother quipped.

"Or," Aimee said, crossing the lawn, "rustic hardwood floors, charming wainscoting, and quaint nooks and crannies."

"Or a big black hole," Summer said, peering around Aimee after she'd marched up the crumbling stoop and flung open the front door.

"Watch your step!" Wilma yelled from somewhere inside.

"Wow." Maggie stood behind Aimee and eyed the broken floor. It looked like someone had dropped a bowling ball through the worn wooden planks.

"I'm so sorry," Wilma said, running into the living room. "The owner promised to get that fixed weeks ago."

"No biggie." Aimee gripped the edges of the door frame with both hands before stretching one leg, then the other, across the gaping hole.

"We appreciate your optimism, sweetie, but don't want it to land anyone in the hospital," Mom said, pulling Summer back by one hand just as she was about to leap through the doorway.

"The back door's perfectly safe," Wilma promised. "Just walk around the side, crawl under the fence, and you're right there."

Maggie looked at her mother as Wilma and Aimee headed toward the back of the house inside and Summer disappeared around the corner of the house outside. "'Crawl under the fence'?"

"Hurry after your sister, please."

For better or worse, the gap in the chain-link metal fence was so big, they were able to duck under it as though they played an early round of limbo rather than crawl. Not that that made the house's peeling pink paint, scraggly, litter-strewn lawn, or waterless concrete bird fountain any more appealing, or Maggie any more eager to pick out her bedroom inside.

"I've conducted a thorough inspection," Aimee said firmly, pulling Maggie into the kitchen once inside.

"In five minutes?"

"My parents have dragged me through dozens of houses. I know what to look for."

"Which is why we dragged you with *us*," Maggie reminded

her playfully. In addition to having regular careers, Aimee's parents bought, renovated, and resold houses without ever living in them, just for fun and some extra money. Maggie had wanted to invite Aimee along because they hadn't really hung out in a while, but because her mother's stress levels might not have handled extra company well, she'd played up Aimee's previous real estate experience.

"Oh, well, this is interesting." Her mother stood frozen in the back doorway, staring at a random pile of dirt and sticks in the middle of the living room.

And they needed all the help they could get.

"It's a handyman's special," Aimee concluded.

Maggie raised her eyebrows. "You'll need to clarify the 'special' part."

"A handyman's special is a cheap house that needs work—in this case, a *lot* of work."

"So it's sort of like a skirt that's been discounted because it's missing buttons? You save money up front but then have to go through all the work of finding the right kind of buttons and sewing them on so the skirt doesn't fall off?"

"Exactly."

"But you wouldn't want to buy said skirt unless it was a fun color, or had pretty ruffles. Its potential would have to be worth the extra work."

"Right."

"So, does the house have potential?"

"Every house that has floors, walls, and a roof has potential."

"Mom, come quick!" Summer shrieked.

Maggie dashed from the kitchen and followed her mother up the dusty narrow staircase, Aimee on her heels. Summer could've been trapped under a collapsed wooden beam, for all she knew, but as she ran, Maggie couldn't help but notice the chipped, discolored paint, stained carpeting, and curious lack of doors throughout the house.

"You can see the sky," Summer said excitedly when they finally found her in a bedroom that was so tiny, Maggie doubted it could even function as a closet and house her relatively small collection of skinny clothes.

Maggie's chin dropped when her eyes finally made it to the ceiling. You could indeed see the sky—right through a boulder-size, open-air, accidental skylight.

"I've seen enough."

"It's not so bad, Mrs. Bean. You just have to use your imagination."

Maggie shook her head slightly at Aimee. She knew she was just trying to be helpful, but her mother wasn't in the mood. She hadn't carried Summer in years, but lifted her now as though she were a toddler, and headed for the door.

"Girls, walk in front of me so I can see you, please."

When they reached the first floor, her mother put Summer down gently and faced Wilma, who stood near a pile of bricks that had once been a fireplace mantel.

"So what do we think?" Wilma asked bravely. "It's a bit of a fixer-upper, but just think of the possibilities you'd have in basically starting from scratch and making it your own."

"This house is a death trap."

Wilma laughed nervously, apparently not getting that their mother wasn't kidding.

"You knew I'd have my girls with me, and you had us come here, anyway."

"I'm sorry." Wilma's smile faded. "The owner said he'd fix the bigger problems."

"Perhaps you should've made sure that happened."

"Perhaps," Wilma said, her voice firmer. "But let me remind you that you're working with a very narrow budget, and your options will be limited."

Maggie resisted the urge to crawl into the bowling-ball hole in the floor by the front door when her mother's mouth fell open and she stared at Wilma, stunned. "We'll be outside," Maggie said, taking Summer's hand and catching Aimee's eye.

"In the car, please, where nothing will fall on you and you won't fall through anything," Maggie's mother called after them.

"Mom seemed pretty mad," Summer said once they were safely inside the car.

"I don't think this is her dream house."

"So?" Summer shrugged. "There are millions of others. This one's just not for us."

Maggie slid down the passenger seat and looked out the window. She wanted to believe it was as simple as that—that their perfect house was out there just waiting to be found—but she was worried. What if it wasn't? What if this was the best they could afford?

"Mags," Aimee said, either not sharing Maggie's concern or sensing the need for a subject change as she grinned and popped her head between the two front seats. "Can we please discuss Ben Parker's cuteness quotient for a minute?"

Maggie widened her eyes and nodded toward the backseat. She could argue later that there really wasn't anything to discuss since addressing Ben's cuteness quotient would be admitting she actually found him cute, which would go against the "no boys" rule. Whatever her feelings on the matter, it definitely wasn't a conversation to be had in front of Summer.

"Don't worry, she's in another world."

Turning slightly, Maggie looked in the side-view mirror and found Summer writing in her notebook and bobbing her head in time to the music on her iPod.

"Sounds like Black Eyed Peas," Aimee guessed.

"In that case, you can discuss Ben Parker's cuteness quotient all you want." Maggie turned back to face Aimee. "But I have nothing to say on the matter."

"Come on, Mags. Not only do his height, dark curly hair, and pretty blue eyes basically define the term, but his personality multiplies it by, like, a million. He's *so* nice. Erica Davis got stung by some bug or fish the other day—which, as reigning Queen of the Day, was just what she needed after her parents told her they were going to Paris and leaving her with a babysitter for the rest of the summer—and he picked her up so she wouldn't have to walk on her hurt foot, carried her to shore, and bandaged the wound."

"That's kind of his job," Maggie said, trying to sound unimpressed even though she'd seen the gentlemanly act herself and thought Ben could teach average guys everywhere a thing or two.

"All the Figure Eights want to marry him. And *you*, lucky girl, get to be with him all day every day."

"Not *with* him, just near him," Maggie corrected. "And I might be near him at night, too."

Aimee leaned farther between the two front seats. "Details, please."

Maggie peeked over the back of the seat to make sure Summer was still occupied, and then turned back to Aimee. "I was invited to a party."

Aimee leaned so far forward, she practically sat on the middle console. "*He* invited you to a party?"

"Well, no. Polly technically invited me, but he was right there and definitely agreed that I should come." Sensing a smile forming, she added, "Not that that matters. Because I have absolutely—"

"Sworn off boys, I know." Aimee shook her head quickly, as though trying to settle a million swirling questions. "So, when's the party? Where? Who'll be there?"

"Saturday night, Polly's house, all the instructors and counselors."

"Mags . . ." Aimee's mouth stayed open, as though she forgot what she was going to say, before snapping shut. She glanced through the driver's side window when a cyclist whizzed by, and turned back to Maggie only when the cyclist reached the end of the road and turned. When she spoke again, her voice lacked its usual range of high-pitched enthusiasm. "A real high school party. Wow. Are you going?"

Maggie paused. The truth was, she hadn't decided. Anytime she thought she had, she immediately came up with a hundred reasons why that was the wrong decision, and changed her mind. When she decided that, yes, she most definitely couldn't pass up this amazing opportunity, the likes of which may never happen again if she turned it down now, she pictured herself standing against a wall in Polly's crowded living room, not talking to anyone because she didn't know anyone besides the other swim instructors who were all busy with their real friends. So then when she decided that no, she most definitely couldn't bear hours of awkward loneliness, the likes of which she'd never have to know if she simply stayed home and read, she pictured herself attempting to abandon her wallflower post in Polly's living room, joining the *American Idol* karaoke audience and cheering on Ben and Jason. "I'm not sure," she finally admitted.

Aimee disappeared from her uncomfortable position between the two front seats, got out of the car, and slid in the driver's seat. "You have to go."

"But—"

"Forget about Peter. Forget about Ben and the dozens of other cute boys who'll be there. Go because last summer, or even a few months ago, you never would've imagined yourself ever having to make this decision at all."

Recalling the countless nights she'd spent in bed with bags of Snickers and Kit Kats and dozens of books, Maggie frowned.

"Go because Anabel Richards and Julia Swanson will fall over in jealousy when we get back to school and talk about your amazing three months with older kids, loud enough for them to overhear."

Temporarily forgetting that, on the chance that her family actually found a house they could afford that wouldn't crumble to a pile of wood and nails once they stepped inside, she might be switching schools before then, Maggie smiled.

"Just *go*." Sighing, Aimee sat back against the seat and carefully traced the Toyota symbol on the steering wheel with one finger. "You should go."

"Come with me."

Aimee shook her head. "I don't think that's a good—"

"Please," Maggie said, growing excited. "We can hang out, talk, and meet new people, together." It was the perfect solution.

"But I wasn't invited. And I'd be the only camper there."

"And I'll be the only junior swim instructor. I'm not exactly one of them either. But everyone will be so distracted, they won't even notice . . . and if they do, we'll just

tell them we're world-renowned visiting Pilates instructors."
Maggie wasn't entirely sure everyone would be too busy to
notice two thirteen-year-olds trying to get in on their good
time, but knew that she and Aimee could handle anything
together.

Aimee considered this. "Well, it *would* be a great opportunity to really evaluate and accurately determine Ben's cuteness quotient."

"It would."

"And the Figure Eights would definitely want me to go
so they can hear all about it. They may even break tradition
and make me Queen of the Day for good news instead of
bad."

Maggie paused. Making the Figure Eights happy wasn't
exactly the reason she wanted Aimee to want to go.

"Who wants breakfast?"

Maggie and Aimee jumped as Maggie's mother leaned
both arms on the driver's side door and stuck her head
through the open window.

"Pancakes, French toast, sausage, bacon." Her mother
licked her lips. "What do you say?"

"You don't eat that kind of stuff," Maggie said, concerned.

"What happened to Wilma?" Summer asked loudly,

still wearing her earphones. "Aren't we looking at more houses?"

"Not today."

They waited for her to elaborate. When she didn't, Aimee climbed over the middle console and into the backseat.

"What's wrong?" Maggie asked after her mother was in the car and struggled—again—to find the right key for the ignition.

"Nothing a buttery blueberry short stack won't fix."

Frowning, Maggie sat back and buckled her seat belt. She didn't know if she'd ever used that exact line, but referring to food as an instant cure-all was certainly something she would've done, once upon a time. For her mother to do so was not only out of character, but especially concerning because Maggie was right there—which meant her mother was so distracted, she'd momentarily forgotten to carefully step around the sensitive issue.

When they finally drove away from the falling-down carnation-pink house, the car filled with stressed silence and Maggie found herself thinking not about their future home and the color of her future bedroom walls, but about Saturday. The idea of spending time with people who knew absolutely nothing about her or where she came from was becoming more appealing by the second.

13.
Arnie gripped Maggie's arm as they stood in the classroom doorway.

Maggie tried to move. When that didn't work, she tried to speak. Both were impossible.

"It's like some kind of freaky fruity wonderland," Arnie finally managed.

The best Maggie could do was nod. Gone were the cardboard cutouts of last week. This week, glittery three-dimensional apples, oranges, bananas, and watermelons, all ten times the size of their real counterparts, dangled from the ceiling. The blinds were drawn and the overhead light was out, leaving the room illuminated by thousands of twinkling white lights zigzagging along the walls. Boxes of crayons and coloring books—including those titled *Molly Goes to the Market* and *Davey Does Dinner*—sat on each desk, and Beach Boys music played from a CD player in the corner of the room. But the most bizarre feature, the thing that had rendered Maggie completely speechless, was the enormous strawberry-shaped disco ball that hung in the center of the room—right above a shiny silver scale.

"I think her blood sugar's dropped to abnormally low levels." Arnie leaned against the door frame for support.

"Isn't it great?" Electra was suddenly behind them, peeking into the room over their shoulders.

"It's something," Maggie marveled.

"Why are you wearing a cape?" Arnie asked suspiciously as Electra squeezed between them.

"Fun, right?" Electra twirled to show off her sparkling superhero outfit, complete with silver cape and enough black spandex to outfit an entire fleet of racing cyclists. "What kid wouldn't want to hang out here with us all day?"

Arnie looked at Maggie. She nodded once.

"Electra, we need to talk," Arnie said carefully.

"You got it." Electra spun toward the snack table. "Let's chat while we hang these streamers and balloons."

"Can we chat before then?"

She turned to them, her smile straightening at the seriousness of Arnie's tone.

"Electra," he began gently, "this is all very nice. Great,

Tricia Rayburn

even. You could probably have a very successful party-planning business serving a fun-loving, health-conscious clientele."

Electra looked at him, then at Maggie. "Thanks."

"It's just, Arnie and I have been doing a lot of brainstorming, and we were sort of hoping we could try out some new ideas with the kids today." The truth was, they hadn't done anything besides discuss website templates, but Maggie wanted to put any potential awkwardness on them, not Electra. "If that's okay with you, of course."

"Oh," Electra said, her shoulders sinking slightly. "I don't know . . . I mean, Pound Patrollers wants you to be involved as much as possible, but this seems rather out of the blue."

Maggie shot Arnie a look. That wasn't an outright no. She agreed wholeheartedly that Electra's way certainly wouldn't lead to weight-loss success, but the kids would arrive any minute. If Electra let them lead the meeting, it wasn't like they actually had a plan.

"What would you talk about?" she asked, untying her cape.

"It's not so much *what* we'd say," Arnie said quickly, "as it is *how* we'd say it."

Electra looked at him, clearly concerned by his vagueness.

"From the heart." Managing to keep a straight face, he held one palm over his chest. "We would speak directly from the heart."

"You know most adults would laugh right now and immediately shoot down your request."

"I do," Arnie said, looking at Maggie, then back at Electra. "Just give us today. Let us try."

"Well . . ." Sighing, Electra removed her cape and tossed it on a nearby desk. "It's no secret I haven't been a kid in a few years—or decades. Maybe you guys know something I don't. Maybe you can reach them in a way a mature, sophisticated adult can't."

Maggie watched Arnie out of the corner of her eye. He stood just inside the classroom, arms crossed loosely across his chest as he awaited Electra's official decision. He seemed coolly confident, as though he'd planned this all along and had just been waiting for the right moment to act. She couldn't recall ever seeing him so sure of himself, and that eased her own worries.

"Okay," Electra said finally, clearly striving to sound more convinced than she felt. "The floor's yours. But know that the second I feel this meeting getting away from you—"

"You'll swoop in and save the day like the superhero you are." Arnie nodded.

"Super*heroine*," she clarified. "And don't think I won't."

"You take care of décor, I'll take care of content," Arnie instructed quietly when Electra flopped into a kid's desk chair and flipped through *Molly Goes to the Market*.

Maggie made a beeline for the room's most troubling decorative touch.

The mammoth silver scale had wheels, but it still took all of her strength to push it across the floor and into the corner of the room. Once it was as far away from the circle of desks as it could get without leaving the room, Maggie grabbed Electra's discarded cape and tied one end to the upper edge of the chalkboard and the other to the top of a window, creating a silver tent around the scale. She ducked underneath and stepped quickly on the scale. Satisfied no one could see in since she couldn't see out, she hopped off and hurried around the classroom, opening all the blinds. When the room was flooded with natural light, she cleared the desks of coloring books and crayons and climbed on and off them, pulling a glittery fruit salad from the ceiling. The disco ball was the last thing to go, and Electra accidentally broke a green crayon as Maggie took the sparkling strawberry with both hands.

She left the overhead light off and twinkling white lights on (because thousands ran up and down the walls, and also because they did make for a warmer, more inviting environment), turned off the bubbly Beach Boys, and joined Arnie at the front desk. She was about to ask what he had up his sleeve, since she thought it might be nice to know exactly what they'd gotten themselves into, when the classroom door swung open.

"Don't worry."

Maggie looked away from the parents and kids and down at her left hand—which Arnie gently squeezed with his right hand.

"Hey, guys," he said, glancing at her quickly before letting go of her hand and heading toward the classroom door. "Welcome back. Matt, Lucy, Gretchen, Paolo, nice to see you. Jack, Katie, Margo, and Alex, glad you could make it."

Maggie knew she should join him in greeting and slapping high fives, but all she could really focus on was the fact that her fingers still tingled. She'd never held a boy's hand before—not that the five-second grasp really qualified as hand-holding—and she certainly hadn't had any reason to mentally prepare for the brief exchange of nervous palm perspiration. On top of which, Arnie's hand had been warm and smooth, not cool and rough the way she'd imagined the hands of her imaginary future boyfriend would be. (Of course, her imaginary future boyfriend did manly things with his hands, like chop wood and build furniture; Arnie played video games and the flute.)

"You all remember the lovely Maggie."

Jolted back to the present moment when she realized Arnie, the kids, and their parents were watching her expectantly, Maggie waved and smiled. "Hi."

"Great." Arnie motioned to the desks and chairs in the middle of the room. "Now, if you'll just take a seat, we'll get this show on the road."

"Arnie, what're we—"

"No pressure," he whispered, opening his laptop, hooking a long black cord into the back, and pulling down a screen behind them. "I'll go first. If you want to go after that, perfect—but don't feel like you have to, *at all.*"

"Okay." Maggie eyed the laptop screen warily. "But what do you mean, you're going first? Going where? To do what?"

"Electra, could you get the blinds, please?"

Maggie watched Electra snap shut each set of blinds. Whatever Arnie was about to do, it had better work.

"We're going back in time," Arnie said quietly, typing quickly, "to get to know one another."

Maggie looked up when giggles filled the room, and then at the screen behind them when Lucy pointed in its direction. "'Arnold Bartholomew Gunderson,'" Maggie read, "'the story of an ordinary boy'?"

Arnie punched one last key and smiled at her. "It's a test run."

"Is that you?" Matt asked boldly, his big grin revealing two deep dimples.

"I wish I could say no." Arnie stepped to the left of the screen and looked at the picture of a happy, laughing, totally naked (except for a diaper) baby, who crawled toward a bottle of milk with his tongue sticking out of his mouth.

"You look like a dog," Lucy said, giggling behind her hand.

"Thanks. I think I was just really hoping Mom remembered to add the Hershey's syrup." He faced the classroom. "Anyway, since we're all going to be spending quite a bit of time together and eventually talking about some pretty important things, I thought you guys should know who you're dealing with."

"A pumpkin!"

"That's right," Arnie said, looking back at the screen. "You're dealing with a pumpkin."

Maggie smiled at the sight of Arnie as a toddler, dressed in an orange felt pumpkin Halloween costume and holding a Snickers bar as big as his arm.

"Pumpkins are cute. So are Superman pajamas, birthday

parties, Christmas mornings, trips to Disney World, and first days of school." Aiming a small white remote at the laptop, Arnie scanned through a dozen equally adorable pictures of him opening presents, eating cake, hugging Mickey Mouse, and boarding school buses. "As you can see, for the first few years of my existence, life was pretty perfect. I was a happy kid doing happy-kid things—playing, going to school, taking fun vacations. My biggest problem was being shot down every time I begged for a chocolate Labrador puppy."

"I want a golden retriever," Margo announced loudly, pouting at her mother.

"We have three cats and a turtle, but I really want a pug," Alex added.

"I feel your pain," Arnie said, and put one hand on his chest to show his sympathy. "But trust me, in the big, grand scheme of things that will probably make more sense when you get a little older, not being able to have a pet is a pretty minor problem."

Maggie glanced quickly around the room. She wasn't exactly sure where Arnie was going with his life-in-photos slideshow, but every kid, parent, and Patrol This group leader watched the screen, completely attentive. No one squirmed in his or her seat or looked toward the door longingly. Whatever Arnie was doing, it was working.

"Behold," he said, pausing dramatically at the first unsmiling shot. "Sixth grade."

"You don't look very happy," Lucy noted.

"I wasn't. In case you can't tell by the fake bookshelf behind me, this is my school picture. And right before the photographer took the shot, I made the very big mistake of accidentally catching my appearance in the monitor behind him." Arnie sighed. "And I didn't like what I saw."

"You *are* wearing a pink shirt," Paolo pointed out. "Didn't you know that was a bad idea when you were getting dressed?"

"Bad shirt, true—but not the problem." Arnie flipped to the next picture of him wearing a puffy blue snowsuit and pouting at the base of a mountain. "A week after that picture was taken, I had to have my annual school physical, where a very grumpy nurse made me get on the scale and then had the nerve to cluck her tongue and tell me to be careful."

"Be careful of *what*?" Gretchen asked incredulously.

"Of growing up—not out."

Several gasps filled the air.

"Adults!" Katie exclaimed. "No offense, Mom."

"Listen, I don't hate the grumpy nurse for saying what she did. Do I think she could've had better delivery? Maybe expressed concern instead of an ominous warning? Sure. But she was right."

Maggie leaned against the teacher's desk and watched more images of Arnie opening presents and eating cake—he was older in these photos, noticeably heavier, and though he still smiled politely for the camera, gone was his childhood glee of earlier photos. In each picture, it was obvious he couldn't wait for the spotlight to turn.

"Somehow, some way—most likely by an unnatural consumption of enormous amounts of potato chips, cookies, bagels, pasta, and quesadillas—I gained a lot of weight in a very short amount of time."

"Why all of a sudden?" Alex asked. "Did something happen?"

"Well . . ." Arnie looked at the floor and tapped the remote lightly against his leg, as though searching for the right words. After a brief moment, he shrugged and looked up. "I wasn't happy. My parents had always worked a lot, but when I was in fifth grade, my dad was made president of his company and my mom started traveling more for her job. So, it was just the nanny and me most of the time. She tried to stop me from snacking at first, but when it seemed to be the only thing that made me feel better, she started baking brownies and peanut butter cookies herself."

Maggie glanced at the parents to see them shake their heads in disapproval.

"And then, of course, that only made things worse. The brownies were delicious, but having one just made me crave more. And I never felt better after eating them—in fact, I usually felt worse, especially if I had a stomachache. And I always felt guilty for eating so much, and then when I started growing out of my clothes, I only felt guiltier, so would eat another plate of brownies, and then another, to try to feel better, which, of course only made me outgrow more clothes."

"Which made you eat more brownies," Katie surmised.

"Exactly. It was like going eighty miles an hour around a traffic circle with no exit ramp."

"So how'd you finally get out?" Katie's mother asked, leaning across the desk.

Arnie clicked the remote, and a new picture filled the screen.

"Whoa," Jack said. "A tornado hit your house?"

"In a sense." Arnie half-laughed, half-sighed. "That pile of wood and velvet is all that remains of a very expensive chair that my parents brought back from their European honeymoon. It was apparently one-of-a-kind, and once belonged to Marie Antoinette."

"I don't recall a tornado ever coming through here," Jack's mother said.

"That's because I only hit one house. Or, one chair." Arnie looked at the screen. "Which I sat in, and broke."

Maggie knew that to remain professional, she needed to appear as though this wasn't the first time she was hearing this story, so even though her head spun and eyes welled with sympathetic tears, she gripped the side of the desk and stared at the screen. In all the time they'd spent together, not once had Arnie ever mentioned breaking the chair. She could imagine how mortified and disgusted with herself she would've been if it'd happened to her, and her heart ached just thinking about Arnie going through such a thing.

"It was pretty much the worst day of my life," he continued bravely. "My parents freaked, grounded me, and immediately signed me up for Pound Patrollers."

Maggie heard people shifting in their seats behind her and pictured the mothers exchanging frowns.

"But, much to my incredible surprise, the worst day eventually led to a whole slew of best days. I hated the idea of going to weight-loss meetings, but I had no choice. So, I went, and made the best of a seemingly bad situation." Arnie clicked ahead to the next picture, the one of him and Maggie in PATROL THIS T-shirts. "And before I knew it, three very amazing things happened: I lost weight, met my best friend, and became a happier, healthier person."

Maggie smiled and hoped her cheeks didn't look as red as they felt when the entire room looked at her.

"And I share all of this with you not because I think my life is especially interesting and worth sharing with anyone who'll listen or enjoys all embarrassing baby pictures, but because I want you to know that I get it." He shot Maggie a small smile. "Maggie and I have both been there, and we get it."

As the kids began firing questions (how much weight did he lose, how did he lose it, did his parents get another chair), Arnie went to the laptop, hit the keyboard, and ended the slideshow. He raised his eyebrows at Maggie, silently asking if she wanted a turn. She shook her head. It wasn't that she didn't want to share—she would, eventually, when she had photos ready—but Arnie's story had resonated. It had broken down walls, and there was no reason to talk more, potentially bore easily distracted kids with too much information, and put the walls back up.

"Believe me," Arnie said, nodding once at her before facing the room, "soon you'll know more about me than I do. But first, I want to get to know *you*. Who you are, how old you are, your favorite movie, what you do for fun, and anything else you want to share. So feel free to grab some water and fruit, and we'll chat."

"Arnie," Maggie said once the kids and parents were occupied by snacks, "that was amazing."

"Very nicely done," Electra said, joining them at the front desk. "I didn't know where you were going at first, but once you got there, those kids were hooked. Now, we just have to get them on the scale."

"Not yet," Arnie said.

Electra looked at him and opened her mouth to protest.

"I mean, if that's okay," Arnie said quickly. "I just think they'll get on the scale when they're ready to get on the scale."

Electra closed her mouth. Apparently there wasn't much to say after Arnie's successful storytelling. "I'm hungry."

"Really amazing," Maggie said again when Electra left for the snack table. "But how come you never told me about the chair?"

He smiled slightly and shrugged. "I was just waiting for the right time."

Before she could ask what that meant, he closed the laptop and headed for the circle of desks and chairs in the middle of the room.

14.

"I'm nervous."

"Me too."

"But you never get nervous," Maggie said, growing even more nervous at the thought of Aimee being nervous. "You're my rock, my pillar of unwavering confidence, my tower of strength in uncomfortable circumstances, my—"

"Mags." Aimee looked at her. "This is a party for counselors—your coworkers, but *my* counselors. Not exactly my area of social expertise."

"Should we just forget it and go get low-fat frozen yogurt instead?"

Aimee shook her head. "Maybe."

They stood on the sidewalk in front of Polly's house, right where Maggie's mother had dropped them off fifteen minutes earlier, each waiting for the other to make the first move. Aimee usually led the way—into classrooms, school functions, club meetings, and basically anything else that involved more than two people and wasn't the library—with Maggie following closely behind, but tonight she'd climbed out of the car and stopped short. Which meant that unless they wanted to stand there for the next three hours, inviting an inevitable barrage of curious looks as other guests came and went, Maggie was going to have to take charge.

"Okay," she said, taking a deep breath and facing the yellow two-story Colonial that was easily three real estate leagues out of that of her family's. "First, we go in and see if we know anyone or if anyone admits to knowing us. After that, we find the kitchen and become very busy with soda and pretzels. Then, depending on how things go up to that point, we find the entertainment, during which we can hopefully just blend in with the upholstery and people-watch until it's time to go."

"Solid plan."

Before she could change her mind, Maggie hooked one arm through Aimee's and headed for the front door. "Do you think we ring the bell?" she whispered once they were on the porch.

Fortunately, a group of loud, laughing guys—soccer instructors, Maggie guessed, though it was hard to be sure without the color-coded camp T-shirts—burst through the door and ran down the porch steps before they could debate the issue.

"Well..." Aimee stared through the open door.

Maggie's heart raced and she silently reminded herself there was no reason to be nervous. It wasn't like they were crashing—Polly had officially invited her. Still, this being not only her first party with high school kids but also her first real party ever, she couldn't help but worry about what she would say and do once they crossed through the doorway. What *did* high school kids say and do at these things, besides make fun of one another while playing *American Idol* karaoke?

"Jason's destroying Celine Dion."

Not much, apparently.

Maggie spun around. Ben stood on the top porch step, holding jumbo-size bags of chips, popcorn, and pretzels.

"We tried to talk him out of it, but he had an entire playlist of greatest hits prepared."

"Celine's had a lot of hits," Maggie said, taking two bags of Doritos from his load as he joined them at the door.

"Which is why the snack replenishment. We may be here for days." Grinning, he turned to Aimee. "I'm Ben."

"I know," Aimee said automatically.

"This is Aimee," Maggie chimed in when Aimee's fair skin turned pink. "She's from camp too."

"The Figure Eights."

Maggie looked at Aimee, surprised at the admission, then at Ben, then back at Aimee.

"I'm a camper," Aimee said sheepishly.

"I thought you looked familiar. Carla's your counselor, right?"

"Right." Aimee looked at her feet, presumably regretting her admission.

"Cool." He smiled and nodded toward the open door. "After you."

"Could I be a bigger idiot?" Aimee whispered as they entered the house. "Social outcast of the century. I might as well just sit on the porch and wait to hear all about your good time."

"'My Heart Will Go On' and other dramatic ballads are being performed in the living room," Ben said, following behind. "Just follow the shrieking, and prepare to cover your ears as you get closer."

"Are you coming?" Maggie asked hopefully. Walking into the crowded room would be a breeze if they were accompanied by camp's most popular instructor.

"Grabbing bowls." He raised his armload of snacks. "Be right there."

Pausing in the hallway, Maggie watched him disappear into the kitchen.

"Oh, and don't forget—no Billy Joel." He stuck his head through the kitchen doorway, grinned, and disappeared again.

"Can I have one of those?" Aimee eyed the bags of Doritos Maggie still held. "At least then maybe it'll look like I have a purpose."

"You have a purpose. *We* have a purpose." Maggie handed her a bag. "To have fun. Period."

Even if she were 100 percent convinced that they really were there just to have fun (which she wasn't, since real fun didn't usually involve the fear of social interaction), she would've been only 5 percent convinced by the time they reached the living room doorway. At least thirty people sat on three overstuffed couches, two armchairs, and the floor, talking and laughing over the center stage entertainment—Jason belting out both the male and female parts of "Beauty and the Beast." So if their ultimate goal was to only blend in with the crowd, actually being part of the crowd would entail climbing, crawling, and squeezing between people who already knew one another and were having fun. And that would certainly draw attention to themselves, which would definitely be anything but fun.

"This is so weird," Aimee said, surveying the room. "Who knew they looked different off camp grounds?"

"Don't be scared."

Maggie spun around, prepared to defend their temporary party paralysis, and found Ben holding two enormous plastic bowls and looking past them into the living room.

"He never ventures far from the flat-screen." He raised both bowls overhead and squeezed gently between Maggie and Aimee. "Harder to read the lyrics that way."

"Where are you going?" Aimee grabbed Maggie's elbow.

"Our purpose is moving."

"He's cute, charming, funny, nice, and everything else," Aimee said, watching Ben carefully navigate the kids sitting on the floor. "But you said you were done with boys."

Maggie held up the Doritos. "Our purpose." She nodded toward the coffee table where Ben was setting down the bowls.

"Oh. Right."

Armed with snacks, joining the crowd turned out to be easier than she'd thought. Spicy Nacho and Cool Ranch were very popular with the counselors, and Maggie and Aimee were quickly surrounded as they emptied their bags into the bowls. Two tennis instructors—easily identified by the Adidas wristbands they always wore—even bowed down like Maggie and Aimee were some kind of junk food–bestowing royalty. No one actually talked to them, but at least they didn't talk *about* them. Plus, the arrival of food had caused a crowd shift on the carpet; once the bags were empty, Maggie and Aimee scurried to the edge of the room and scored a patch of floor with a great view of the entertainment.

"This isn't so bad." Maggie giggled as Jason's voice cracked and he squatted in front of the TV to read the lyrics running along the bottom of the screen.

"I guess." Aimee leaned toward Maggie. "Do you want to maybe check out the rest of the house? And come back in a little bit?"

"Totally," Maggie said. She was about to get up from the floor when Jason hit another painfully high note. The crowd howled, and Maggie joined their applause.

"Mags?"

Maggie glanced up to see Aimee standing, arms crossed over her stomach and looking like she'd rather be anywhere else. "Can we just watch him finish? He has to be almost done."

Aimee frowned, looked around as though worried someone was going to catch her doing something she shouldn't, and slowly lowered herself back to the floor.

As Jason crooned, Maggie scanned the room and saw Polly holding hands and laughing with Carter, the basketball instructor (easily identified by the way he towered over everyone, even sitting down), three guys holding a loud, heated debate near an enormous fish tank, and an intriguing game of snack popping (a group of guys tossing popcorn, pretzels, and anything else they grabbed from the bowls without looking into each other's mouths). She was so enjoying the off-stage entertainment, she almost didn't notice when Jason finished a song, bowed, guzzled a can of Mountain Dew in preparation for his next performance— and was suddenly joined by Ben.

"Dude," Jason said into the microphone as Ben tried to wrestle it gently from his grasp, "I'm not fin—"

"Everyone, let's give Mr. Dion a big round of applause, shall we?" Ben encouraged once in full control of the microphone. "If only music execs had discovered him first."

Maggie laughed and clapped as the room exploded in applause and whistles. Having no choice but to accept his favorable reception, Jason curtsied and blew kisses before reluctantly vacating the stage.

"Sing us a song, piano man!"

"Sing us a song tonight!"

Ben faced the cheering counselors and instructors—all of whom had immediately stopped debating, snack popping, and doing their best to tune out the music when he took the microphone—scratched his chin, and pretended to consider the request.

"It's a crowd-pleaser, apparently," Maggie explained to Aimee.

"Great," Aimee said flatly.

"If you insist," Ben finally said. He turned toward the TV, picked up the PlayStation controller, and quickly hit a bunch of buttons. When an animated version of himself swaying in time to the song's beginning chords appeared on the screen, he turned back to the room and smiled.

"He's adorable," Aimee said almost reluctantly, shooting Maggie a pointed look, as though the observation was something Maggie should pay attention to.

He was—swearing off boys hadn't rendered her blind—but Maggie let Aimee's look slide without responding. Because she didn't want to notice. She didn't want to spend one second thinking about his dark wavy hair, his perpetual, contagious smile, or the indisputable fact that jeans, a blue T-shirt, and red flip-flops had never looked better on anyone else. She didn't want to spend one second thinking about how his good looks were only amplified a million times by his easygoing nature, sincerity, and kindness, which had become very apparent even in the short time she'd known him. She didn't want to spend one second thinking about the fact that every single person in the room—male and female—clearly loved him and wanted to be his best friend. Because she knew if she spent just one second thinking about any of those things, the unbreakable pact she'd made with herself might begin to crack. And then one second would turn into minutes, then hours, then days—and she'd already lost enough time thinking about a boy.

So, instead of thinking about whether she might like him under different circumstances, she thought about how she wished she could simply *be* more like him. Apparently, he'd performed the song more than once, because he knew the words without having to follow the lyrics on the screen, and that enabled him to work the room of fans effortlessly. He fell to his knees and jumped back up for dramatic emphasis, mingled with the crowd as much as the microphone cord would allow, and even sang in tune. Losing weight and doing well on the school swim team had certainly boosted Maggie's confidence, but only enough to not feel completely out of place at any given point; she wondered what it would feel like to be the center of attention and not worry—or even care—what people thought of her being there.

"How about that house tour now?" Aimee asked loudly so Maggie could hear over the booming applause as Ben belted his last note.

"You got it." Maggie clapped and grinned as Ben bowed to his adoring fans. "Let's just make sure he doesn't do an encore."

"Maggie—"

"And now to really get things rolling, how about we try something new?"

Forcing herself to look away from Ben, Maggie turned to Aimee. "Five more minutes?"

"I thought we'd pick up the pace a little, put some fun into the funky that Jason has so masterfully turned these get-togethers into."

"Mags," Aimee said, leaning toward Maggie. "This is actually a little weird for me, and I was kind of hoping to talk to you about some stuff—"

"And what better way to do that than with the help of the Queen of Pop herself?"

Aimee frowned as a new song started and the room erupted in a fresh wave of applause.

"Now, Madonna is too big for the efforts of just one man, so I'm going to need a little help."

"Right, let's go," Maggie said, watching Ben as she climbed to her knees. Aimee clearly had something to say, and there was no way Maggie was going to hear it over Madonna.

"So I'd like to invite a lovely Camp Sound Viewer to the stage. She's fairly new to our crazy family, but has already made quite an impression."

"Ready?" Maggie climbed to her feet and held out one hand to help Aimee up.

"Miss Maggie?"

Suddenly wishing she'd opted to crawl toward the door rather than stand and walk, Maggie froze.

"Care to vogue?"

Maggie turned her head slowly to see Ben grinning and looking at her expectantly. "Actually," she began, thankful for the living room's dim lighting as her face burned, "I was just about to—"

"Sing some warm-up scales?" Ben shook his head. "You don't need them."

"C'mon, Maggie!" Polly called from across the room. She clapped and whistled, and the rest of the room quickly joined in.

"You only have one microphone," she said nonchalantly. "I don't want to *steal your thunder*."

Ben's grin broadened. "I'm happy to share."

As the cheers and whistles grew louder, Maggie's head spun. What was the worst that could happen? So what if she sang out of tune and messed up the words? Wasn't that the point? On top of which, she'd be singing out of tune and messing up the words with Ben, who could do no wrong in the eyes of his thirty closest friends. Surely his unwavering support would balance out her bad performance. And, on the other hand, if she left the room as intended, she'd be forever known as the scared new girl who'd turned down the chance to share the spotlight with a camp icon.

Heart racing, Maggie looked at Aimee, who still sat on the floor. Aimee's shrug and half smile wasn't quite the support Maggie hoped for, but it was enough for her to turn toward Ben and begin carefully stepping around people en route to the TV.

"There's my girl," Ben said into the microphone.

Maggie shook her head in (almost) mock embarrassment as she stood next to him.

"The words are on the bottom of the screen, and the yellow arrow tells you if you're on pitch." He held the microphone away so only she heard him. "They'll hardly hear us over themselves, but just remember, you're among friends."

As it happened, Ben incorporated spontaneous dance moves into his "Vogue" performance, making Maggie laugh so hard, she could barely read the lyrics through the tears welling in her eyes, and rendering anything resembling actual singing basically impossible. But she tried and, after a while, even forgot to be nervous. The counselors and instructors eventually started singing along, and they all became one big, loud, untalented chorus. When Ben casually slung one arm across her shoulder toward the end of the song, Maggie glanced to where she'd left Aimee to make sure that, as her best friend and witness, she could confirm everything that happened later.

And nearly choked on the lyrics and fell off the imaginary stage when Aimee wasn't there.

Maggie tried to shrug out of Ben's arm, but he pulled her back gently. Deciding that Aimee had probably just gone outside for air and silently vowing to find her as soon as the song was over, Maggie smiled at Ben and returned to her thirty new friends.

15. On her next visit to Arnie's lake house, Maggie bounded up the porch steps and knocked on the door without hesitation. Gone was her trepidation about revisiting the scene of the Peter Applewood Incident. In fact, as she opened the door, the only thing related to that day that occurred to her was the fact that thinking about it no longer made her want to curl into a ball and cry.

"Hey, Mag—"

"How beautiful is today?"

Coming into the living room Arnie looked curiously at her, then past her, as though evaluating the day. "Do you want, like, a number or something?"

"The sun's out, the sky's blue, and we have the whole afternoon to hang out." Maggie put her hands on her hips and turned slightly to face the lake. "What could be better?"

Arnie shrugged. "We could have the whole day to hang out. But that won't work because I still have to jog one hundred miles, climb seven mountains, and find a cure for cancer."

Maggie turned back to Arnie and frowned. "Parents still bumming you out?"

"No more than usual," he said lightly. "Want to come in?"

"I was thinking about staying outside."

"Outside?"

"Your wireless works in the yard, right? We could take your laptop and notes and hang out in the Adirondack chairs out back. Unless your parents are home, in which case we can totally hide out in your room to work and sneak out later."

"The parents are in Madrid. Their absence doesn't get me out of my daily schedule—because the staff now takes random video footage of me doing everything I'm supposed to do, which they e-mail to my parents as proof—but it does enable us to move freely about the property."

"Random video footage?"

"I couldn't make it up if I tried." He held the door open for her. "I'll grab the stuff and meet you out back."

The easiest way to get to the backyard was through the kitchen, which Maggie headed for with ease. She paused only briefly outside the door, when a quick image of her and Peter talking while sitting on the island stools flashed through her mind, but then she simply replaced that uncomfortable mental picture with one of singing with Ben. Smiling, she entered the kitchen and strolled toward the French doors as though the most catastrophic thing to have ever occurred there were the mindless consumption of greasy pizza and sugary soda. Once outside, she plopped in an Adirondack chair overlooking the lake, closed her eyes and, for the thousandth time that day, replayed the events of the night before.

She'd stopped to rewind at the same spot she'd stopped to rewind at each of the thousand times before—when she'd left Ben in search of Aimee and found her sulking on the front porch outside, which she chose not to replay since the awkward conversation and silent car ride that had followed negated everything that happened before—when Arnie flopped in the chair next to hers.

"Fresh watermelon?"

"I *love* watermelon." Maggie took the Baggie of fruit and popped two cubes in her mouth.

"If only I'd known I would never have wasted time on Soy Crisps and granola." Arnie flipped open the laptop screen and started typing. "Anyway, I've done a few things since last week. Tell me what you think."

Maggie popped two more watermelon cubes in her mouth and leaned across the chairs' wide arms. "Are you wearing cologne again?"

Arnie paused.

"It smells nice."

"Thanks." He cleared his throat and turned the laptop toward her. "So, I posted my Arnold Bartholomew Gunderson slideshow online, and came up with endearingly funny captions."

"That was *so* great last week. The kids and parents were totally hooked."

Arnie smiled. "I also added all the basic technical stuff Pound Patrollers insisted on—food pyramid, calorie converter, body-mass index calculator, and exercise chart—but made the link smaller than all the others."

"So kids don't get scared off as soon as they hit the site." Maggie nodded. "Good thinking."

"Then I added some graphics and backgrounds, all simple but fun, and started a list of things we might want to include."

"Like music playlists? Great songs to work out to? And fun, easy, healthy recipes? Oh, and maybe we can have a contest spanning a few months, and whoever reduces their body-mass index most successfully, or somehow makes the biggest change toward a healthier, happier life, wins a bike? Or a canoe?"

"A canoe?"

"Rowing's great for the chest, arms, back, quads, abs, and pretty much everything else."

"Great idea." Arnie pulled up a spreadsheet and added the contest to the list of ideas.

Maggie popped the last of the watermelon, leaned back in her chair, and looked out at the lake. "This is going to be awesome. Pound Patrollers won't know what's coming."

"They'll probably want us to quit school so we can help kids all around the country lose weight full-time."

"Definitely."

"I've actually posted some of this stuff online already, so people can actually visit it and nose around, and we're getting way more hits than I thought we'd ever get, let alone so early on."

"Of course we are! With your technological genius, how could we not?"

"Right." Arnie laughed, then paused. "So what's with the mood?"

"What mood?" Maggie smiled as a father-son fishing team reeled in a big catch. "I'm not in a mood."

"Yes, you are. An off-the-charts, never-seen-before, amazingly good mood."

"Am I?" Unable to stop grinning, Maggie casually covered her mouth with one hand.

"Did something happen? Did you win the lottery? Did Harvard send you a really early preapplication acceptance packet?"

Suddenly slightly uncomfortable that her happiness was so abnormally noticeable—and not wanting to delve into the real reason why—Maggie shrugged. "I just had a good week at work."

"A good week at work. My parents have a good week at work and they collapse in bed, too exhausted from the exertion of the good week to appreciate it."

Maggie looked at him. "The same parents who also ask the staff to secretly videotape you?"

"Point taken."

"So what do you need me to do?" she asked, determined to detract attention from her by focusing on the task at hand.

"Well, we can both brainstorm healthy snacks and songs, and then I had another idea that I wanted to run by you."

"Run away."

"I don't know if you're going to like it."

"If you thought of it, I'm sure I'll love it."

"It definitely makes the site way more personal than we ever thought we'd want it to be."

"Arnie. We already have naked baby pictures of you on there. How much more personal can it get?"

"As personal as a diary?"

"A diary."

"Not like a 'I went to the mall and bought three shirts and a pair of sneakers before coming home and watching TV with my parents and calling it a day' kind of diary. More of a 'I went to this amazing Italian restaurant and practically died when they brought out the basket filled with soft, warm rolls and buttery slices of garlic bread and knew it was either keep drinking water, salivate all over the table, or commit to a lifetime of crunches if I even touch one piece' kind of diary."

"Huh." Maggie considered this.

"We could do it any way you want. We can take turns, do it daily, weekly, or stick to a flexible schedule of whenever a food challenge presents itself, or whatever. I just thought it would be helpful for kids to know that we still face these really hard issues sometimes but do our best to deal with them."

"It's a great idea." She paused.

"But?"

"It's just . . ." Potentially completely and totally embarrassing, especially if the wrong web surfer stumbled upon it. It'd be bad enough if Ben ever happened to find out about her past, but there was no way she wanted him to ever know that her past still affected her present—that it could still be a struggle to pass up candy, cookies, and cake, that she had to consciously think about passing up on those things while most people effortlessly took them or left them. "It's just a lot of information. And probably a lot of time. Work's keeping me pretty busy, you know."

"Oh." Arnie looked at his laptop screen. "Okay. Well, it was just an idea."

"It's a great idea," Maggie reassured. "And I think kids would really love it. But maybe we can tackle it later? Like as a groundbreaking phase two of the website development?" Surely she could come up with a better reason for not participating by phase two—whatever and whenever that was.

"Sure." Arnie shrugged. "Sounds good."

"And I'll definitely do the Margaret Ann Bean slideshow," she offered brightly. "I have, like, *thousands* of embarrassing pictures I'll happily put up for the benefit of our kids." Carefully and selectively, of course.

"Right. That'll be good."

Maggie watched Arnie absently scroll down the spreadsheet still on his laptop screen. "You okay?"

"Of course." He sat up straighter in the chair. "Shall we start coming up with snacks that sound way better than they taste?"

"Actually," Maggie said, leaning toward him, "what if we played hooky instead?"

"Hooky?"

"Working hooky, if we must." She glanced at the sparkling lake. "It's just such a great day. Why don't we brainstorm on your parents' boat?"

"Well, because of the random video footage, for one."

"We've taken their boat out before."

"With Peter and Aimee, with their permission. If they found out we took it out without asking, you'd end up one friend short."

"No problem." Maggie shrugged. "I just thought it'd be nice. But it's nice right here, too."

"It *would* be nice." Arnie looked across the lake, then back at the house.

"Not a big deal, though," Maggie said, watching his knee start bouncing nervously.

He gathered papers, closed manila folders, and shut the laptop.

"Arnie?"

He stood, piled everything on the chair, and held out his hand.

She grinned. "Really?"

"It's docked, fueled, and ready to go. And my parents are in *Spain*."

She took his hand, jumped to her feet, and practically jogged to keep his pace as they crossed the backyard.

"We just need to be back kind of early to meet Pete."

Still holding Arnie's hand, she stopped short, accidentally yanking him back.

"What's up?"

"Pete," she repeated. "As in Peter? Your cousin Peter?"

"And your friend Peter? The one and the same." He looked at her curiously, as though wondering why she'd think there'd be any other.

She fought the urge to sink to the ground. For some reason, despite last night, the way she'd breezed through the kitchen earlier and her amazingly good mood, the thought of seeing him again had hit her like a tree branch, knocking the wind out of her. "Maybe we should go on the boat another time."

Arnie's face fell. "Why? What's wrong?"

"House hunting," Maggie said automatically, still trying

to process her feelings. "I just remembered Mom lined up a few showings this afternoon. I should probably be there."

"What about hanging out the entire afternoon?"

Maggie looked at him and smiled, trying to appear casual so her reaction didn't freak him out as much it freaked her out. "I'm really sorry. But I promise to work on the website stuff tonight and e-mail you what I find."

"Okay, I guess."

She glanced down, suddenly aware that their hands were still clasped. "So I'm going to go."

He looked down, realized the same thing, and gently let go of her hand.

"Sorry about this," she called over her shoulder as she hurried across the lawn. "We'll talk later!"

She'd reached the back porch and was about to sprint up the steps, since, for some reason she'd have to figure out later, she couldn't seem to get away from the house and the possibility of seeing Peter Applewood in person fast enough, when Arnie called her name. She spun around, breathless, and saw him standing exactly where she'd left him.

He opened his mouth, about to speak, then closed it, shoved his hands in his shorts pockets, and looked at the ground. "Can we do it some other time?" he finally asked, looking up at her. "Go out on the boat together, I mean?"

Maggie smiled. "Absolutely," she said, relieved that he hadn't asked about her bizarre behavior. "See you."

As she dashed through the French doors and across the kitchen, she kept her eyes lowered to avoid accidentally looking at anything that would bring back that night. It wasn't until she was out of the house and sprinting across the front lawn that she realized she was humming the melody to "Vogue."

16.

"Maggie, I don't feel very good about this."

"Dad, it's fine. I promise."

Her dad sighed and leaned forward to peer through the windshield. "But it's dark as night out there—never mind the fact that it's so early it basically *is* night."

"They're just clouds. It's not even raining." Maggie eyed the dashboard clock. "And I'm wet all day, anyway. What's a little rain?"

"A little rain is nothing. An earth-shaking thunderstorm with torrential downpour—which is about the tamest pending scenario, from the looks of that sky—is reason for me to drive you back home."

"Dad, it's my job. The swim instructors have to be early to do laps so that we're ready to go by the time the campers arrive." It wasn't an outright lie—Jason and Ben did warm-up laps to make them ready to go by the time the campers arrived.

"Maggie, honey, I would bet a million dollars that *no one's* going in that water today."

"Dad, if you had a million dollars, I'd quit this job tomorrow and spend the rest of the summer sorting your stacks of money into neat, organized piles while lounging by our luxurious in-ground pool." Which was safe to say, since if her dad really had a million dollars to bet with, they'd never have any trouble buying a house.

"If you see *one* bolt of lightning, or, forget that—if you feel *one* droplet of rain—promise me you'll get out of the water and run like mad to the nearest shelter."

"Run like mad." Maggie nodded. "Got it."

"Your mother's going to kill me."

Maggie leaned across the console to kiss his cheek. "Thanks, Dad." She opened the car door and slid from the front seat.

"At least take my umbrella!" he called just as she was about to slam the door shut.

Maggie grabbed the umbrella, closed the door, and walked quickly to the camp entrance. Once certain she was no longer visible from the parking lot—so her dad couldn't mistake her speed for fear of threatening elements—she started jogging, then running, then sprinting toward the trail that led to the beach.

She understood her father's concern—it was definitely a gray, ugly day, and the sky did look angry enough to hurl lightning bolts. When she'd wakened that morning and looked outside her bedroom window, her heart had fallen at the sight of the sky that was dark with clouds and not just lingering night. She'd briefly considered climbing back under the covers for an extra hour of sleep, but after spending all weekend thinking about Friday night at Polly's house, she'd decided she couldn't wait one extra minute to get to camp.

By the time she reached the trail, her heart pulsated in her ears and her lungs felt like they were one breath away from exploding in her chest. She would've slowed down to keep from passing out, but the sky roared suddenly above her, like it was tearing right down the middle. She flew through the woods, stumbling slightly over small rocks and keeping her arms out to push away branches. Halfway down the trail, tiny droplets sprinkled onto her head and face. When she emerged from the trail's mouth and onto the beach, the tiny droplets gave way to unrelenting sheets, instantly soaking her hair, shorts, and T-shirt. The sand slowed her pace, which she took advantage of to try to open her dad's umbrella.

"Madge!"

Sure she was hearing things, Maggie glanced up from the umbrella handle and squinted through the rain.

"Madonna!"

Unable to see five feet in front of her, Maggie spun to the left, then to the right, trying to pinpoint the voice.

"The lifeguard stand!"

She could barely make it out, but shot in its general direction. She didn't see the familiar white legs and platform until they were right in front of her, and didn't see Ben until he waved both arms in the air.

"What are you doing?" The rain was so loud, he practically shouted as she crawled in between the legs of the lifeguard stand and joined him underneath.

"Wondering why on earth I didn't go back to bed," she practically shouted back.

"Isn't it awesome?"

"Awesome. Right." She dropped her backpack to the sand and leaned against one of the legs to catch her breath, noticing as she did so that it was actually dry under the stand. Blue plastic CAMP SOUND VIEW ponchos hung from each side of the lifeguard stand like tarps and blocked out the rain. Two life preservers sat at a ninety-degree angle against each other (with the back cushions pushed against one of the stand legs) in a makeshift chair. In the middle of the square patch of sand was Ben's backpack, on top of which sat a bagel, a carton of orange juice, and a worn copy of *The Great Gatsby*. "Did you do all this?" she asked, forcing herself to look away from the book.

"I love summer storms." He lifted one edge of the poncho that hung from the front of the stand and looked toward the churning water. "There's nothing like them."

Maggie opened her mouth to agree, but was quickly silenced by another enormous boom overhead.

"You must be freezing." He dropped the edge of the tarp, grabbed his backpack, and pulled out a towel and sweatshirt. "Here."

"No, that's okay, I—"

"Madge." He looked at her, clearly amused by her unnecessary refusal.

"Thank you." She took the towel and sweatshirt gratefully.

"So you didn't say why you're here so early," he said as she wrung out her hair, shorts, and T-shirt. "On early Erin duty again?"

"Not exactly." She bent over, flipped her hair so it fell in front of her face, and toweled it dry to buy time. Her original plan had been simply to say she was up early and felt like a morning swim—she had to stay in shape for the swim team, after all. That reason no longer made much sense, since one look outside would've suggested she save the morning swim for another day, and thinking she'd have at least the walk from the parking lot to the beach to come up with a new one, she hadn't thought of anything better.

"Summer storm watcher too?"

Maggie stood upright and flipped her hair back. "Amateur. Can you tell?"

"Don't be offended if I say yes."

"Definitely not." She smiled, thankful that he didn't press the issue.

"Well, have a seat and make yourself at home." He motioned to the life preserver chair. "Are you hungry? Do you want my bagel?"

"No thanks." She pulled his green sweatshirt over her head and tried not to notice the way it smelled like a combination of laundry detergent and deodorant. "Wow—Dartmouth," she said, noting the white block letters across her chest as she sat in the life preserver chair.

"Only four years and two months away." He took one more look outside before sitting on the sand. "Not that I'm counting."

"So you're . . ."

"Going to be a sophomore."

"Planning ahead—I like it." Maggie nodded approvingly. "And colleges don't get much more impressive than Dartmouth."

"Have you been? Taken a tour of the campus?"

Maggie laughed. "I'm planning ahead, but haven't quite reached the campus tour portion of my life itinerary. That's next summer."

"So you're . . ."

"Going into eighth grade," she admitted reluctantly. She would've considered aging herself at least into ninth grade, but there was really no point since he already knew how old she was from her first day of work.

"You seem older." He looked at her about five seconds longer than anyone else would've in the same conversation before draining his orange juice. "Anyway, Dartmouth's a great school. Amazing academics, but equally if not more importantly, amazing location. Mountains, lakes, national forests. It's pretty much paradise."

"I can't *wait* to go to college."

"It's always something, huh?"

"What do you mean?"

"Well, when we're really little, we can't wait to do so

many things—ride a bike, have friends sleep over, see PG-13 movies. And then, with each thing we're able to do, there are, like, a dozen new ones we can't wait for."

"Driving would be good."

"Driving would be *very* good." He laughed.

"But college is definitely one of the big ones. Leaving your parents, living with strangers, figuring out what you're going to do with the rest of your life."

"Kind of scary."

"But also really exciting." Maggie shivered—either from the chill of the rain or the idea of everything that was to come—and wrapped her Dartmouth-covered arms more tightly around her.

"Kind of like this," he said, looking up.

Maggie jumped and nearly slid off her life preserver chair when another boom ripped through the sky—and then another, and another.

"Awesome." Ben grinned. "It's so close."

"Is this safe? For us to be out here, I mean?" She'd never feared thunderstorms, but then she'd never really been outside, right smack in the middle of one before.

"Come here, storm chaser." He stood on his knees and shuffled across the sand to the blue poncho hanging from the front of the stand.

It wasn't quite the reassuring answer she'd hoped for, but she shuffled on her knees after him, anyway.

"Ready?"

She had no idea if she was ready. He held one edge of poncho in his hand, and she didn't know what would happen when he lifted it (she had visions of a sudden air vacuum sucking the lifeguard stand up and into the stratosphere, like Dorothy's house in *The Wizard of Oz*), so there was no way to know what she was supposed to be ready for. But she nodded, anyway.

As Ben pulled the poncho to one side, she closed her eyes and braced for impact. She slowly opened one eye at a time when the biggest impact was a light spray on her face. "Oh," she breathed when both eyes were open and actually focused ahead of her. "Oh, wow."

The rain still came down in torrents, and the sky boomed every few seconds, like the Jolly Green Giant bowled with boulders. Strong gusts of wind caused a fine mist to swirl a foot above the water's surface, and the gray clouds moved and shifted quickly, unpredictably. But the best part, the thing that made her breath catch in her throat, was the lightning. Dozens of long, jagged bolts crackled through the sky and shot into the horizon, one right after the other. Her dad would've freaked if he saw her now, huddled under a lifeguard stand with a boy, way closer to electrified shards of light than any human ever should be, and she knew she should probably be scared—but she wasn't. She'd never seen anything so beautiful.

"Amazing, right." He wasn't asking a question.

She nodded.

"Maggie," he said without looking away from the horizon.

"Yes."

"Maybe we should hang out sometime."

She casually wiped her eyes, as though their sudden widening was due to an onslaught of sea spray.

"Outside of camp, I mean. If you want."

Quickly deciding that given the lightning, rain, and extraordinarily intense atmospheric conditions she would just have to process how this affected her big life plan later, she nodded again. "Maybe we should."

"Good." They still stood on their knees, and he rocked gently to one side to bump against her.

"Just as long as my showing up here doesn't count as stealing your thunder," she said, bumping him back. "We'll save that for the singing."

17. The small white ranch sat on a quiet, tree-lined street in a lovely neighborhood whose residents waved and smiled as Maggie and her family drove by. The front lawn, though not very large, was green and neat, with pink, purple and white pansies lining the walkway to the door. The mailbox was in the shape of a sailboat, and a yellow homemade birdhouse hung from a branch of a towering maple tree. It was cute, clean and, at least from the exterior, just about perfect—which meant the interior was fatally flawed.

"I think I'm going to sit this one out." Maggie stretched her legs across the backseat as Summer and her parents climbed out of the car.

"But this is *family* house-hunting day," Summer reminded her. "All for one and one for all."

"I know. And that was really great five hours ago, but I'm tired now. Plus, this is the seventh house. If the first six didn't do it, I doubt this one will."

"Maggie." Her dad stuck his head through the open window and looked at her over the top of his sunglasses. "It's the seventh and last house. Surely you can summon the energy to do one final walkthrough."

"How about I'll do one final walkthrough if the house warrants it? All you have to do is stand in the front doorway and whistle, and I'll come running. Otherwise, I'll meet you here."

"It's been a long day." Looking exhausted and not particularly optimistic herself, Maggie's mother lifted her arms overhead and stretched.

"Fine." Her dad pulled away from the window. "But just remember this could be your most perfect house, and you could be missing the chance to convince us that it's *our* most perfect house."

"It's a risk," Maggie admitted. "Mom, may I please use your cell phone while you're touring?"

Her mother handed her the cell phone and leaned through the window to kiss the top of her head.

Maggie watched them head for the front door. She would've been more inclined to go inside if her dad hadn't been with them. He'd joined them on this house-hunting trip as a result of their last (when Wilma had shown them the house of holes), after which Mom had thrown out every listing and real estate pamphlet she'd printed or picked up over the past few weeks. Over dinner that night, she'd insisted that there were just no decent houses in their price range, and declared themselves eternal renters. So, Dad relieved her of the somewhat solo mission; he researched and found a new realtor and listings, took the day off from work to accompany them, and even made them breakfast in bed that morning so that they started the day as fresh and fulfilled as possible. He'd been cool as a cucumber all day, from suggesting that Summer leave her backpack of amenity analysis in the car to alleviate any additional pressure, to calmly shepherding a particularly ferocious trio of barking, nipping shih tzus into a closed-off sunroom while touring house number three. Throughout the day he'd held doors open, talked and joked easily with the realtor, and held her mom's hand when he didn't have his arm around her waist.

Which had made it okay for Maggie to take a much-needed break. After three days of casual conversation following Monday's summer storm (which was all they had time for since, not wanting to overdo it, Maggie had opted out of early morning swims), Ben had approached her while she stacked inner tubes and asked if she wanted to check out the local bookstore's author series on Saturday night. She'd said yes immediately, her excitement obliterating any memory of the already-planned day of family house hunting. There was no way to get out of it—any excuse she might've used, like sudden stomach flu or Patrol This work, would've also been reason to not go out later that night—so she'd walked dutifully through dozens of rooms, her nerves making it really difficult to appreciate things like original hardwood floors and custom-made built-ins.

"Aimee," Maggie practically burst when the phone stopped ringing. "Thank goodness you're home."

"Yup, I'm home."

"I feel like I haven't seen you in forever. We have so much to talk about." Though she'd spotted Aimee across the beach a few times throughout the week, Aimee had been so busy with the Figure Eights and Maggie had been so busy with campers, they hadn't actually spoken. Maggie had tried calling at night after camp, but received the answering machine every time.

"We do? What's up?"

Maggie sat up straight in the backseat and faced the front of the house to monitor the proximity of potential eavesdroppers. "I think I'm going on a date tonight."

"You think?"

"Well, it's kind of hard to tell. When Ben and I were hanging out Monday morning—"

"Ben the swim instructor?"

"Yes."

"You were hanging out with Ben the swim instructor Monday morning?"

"Yes, but not, like, intentionally. I went for an early swim, and he and Jason always work out in the morning. But Jason wasn't there because he was actually smart and stayed home because of the rain, so it was just Ben and I, huddled under the lifeguard stand watching the storm. Did you know summer thunderstorms are amazingly beautiful? I didn't. I mean, I always liked a good thunderstorm, but I'd never really just sat and watched one before. The whole horizon was on fire, and—"

"Maggie."

"Sorry." Maggie took a deep breath. "Anyway, that morning Ben said he thought maybe we should hang out sometime, and on Thursday he asked if I'd want to hang out tonight."

"And you said yes."

"And I said yes. And I really wanted to tell you, because even though I don't know for sure it's a date, if it *is*, there are so many things to discuss! What I should wear, what he might be thinking, where we might go, what we might talk about, and perhaps the biggest question of all: Why he asked *me* out of all of his adoring female fans at camp."

"That's a lot of questions."

Maggie paused before launching into the dozen different outfit combinations she was contemplating. Not only did Aimee not sound especially excited, she barely sounded like she heard what Maggie was saying. "Aim, is everything okay?"

"What about your whole swearing-off-boys thing?" Aimee asked suddenly, her voice tense and louder than normal.

"I'm not marrying the guy," Maggie said defensively. "In fact, I haven't even really thought about whether I like him like that."

"But up until a few weeks ago, you were totally head over heels for Peter Applewood. That's all I heard about all day, every day. Peter Applewood's *so* cute. Peter Applewood's *so* nice. I hope Peter Applewood asks me to the prom—in *five* years. Then the summer comes and you have zero interest in meeting any boys—because you're still hung up on stupid Peter Applewood—and now you're hanging out with the most popular guy at camp. It just seems a little out of the blue."

"Wow. Sorry for the curveball. For some reason I thought you'd be excited for me, happy that maybe I could actually get over stupid Peter Applewood and move on with my life. I had no idea it'd make you mad."

"Sorry," Aimee huffed, not sounding sorry at all. "But just so you know, you're not the only one with things going on."

Maggie opened her mouth to ask what that meant when two long piercing whistles made her cringe. She looked out the window to see Summer waving frantically from the front stoop.

"I mean, maybe you could ask how *I* am every once in a while. Maybe you could stop thinking about yourself long enough to wonder if anyone else in the world has problems."

Summer whistled again before hopping off the stoop and running toward the car.

"While I'd really like to continue this lovely conversation," Maggie said tersely as Summer neared listening distance, too taken aback to try to figure out where Aimee's attack was coming from, "I have to go."

"Of course you do. Tell your boyfriend I said hi."

Maggie stared at the blank cell phone screen. Aimee had never hung up on her before. She and Aimee had never fought before. She wasn't sure if what had just happened qualified as a fight, but it was certainly the closest they'd ever come to it, and Maggie had no idea why.

"Maggie," Summer said breathlessly, reaching the car. "This is it."

Maggie looked at the blank cell phone screen for another second, willing it to flash with Aimee's number as she called back. When it didn't, she turned to Summer. "What's it?"

"This house." She beamed. "Not too big, not too small. And *so* pretty."

"That's great, Sum. But I doubt that means—" She stopped when she spotted her parents standing on the front stoop. They were smiling from ear-to-ear, and waved for Summer and Maggie to join them. "Really?"

Summer nodded and opened the door for Maggie to get out.

"Are you serious?" she asked her glowing parents when she reached the stoop.

"See for yourself." Her dad pushed the front door open.

"Three bedrooms, two bathrooms, living room, family room, dining room, and kitchen with breakfast nook." Her mom listed the highlights as they moved into the house. "Perfect amount of space."

Maggie followed Summer and her parents through the

entire house. Because every one of her family members was excited, she managed to temporarily block out the fact that she'd be hanging out with Ben in three hours, and that her best friend in the whole world had just hung up on her for no apparent reason. The house was bigger than it looked from the outside, and she appreciated every inch—the shiny hardwood floors, living room fireplace, stainless-steel appliances, marble countertops, tiled bathroom floors, and walk-in closets in every bedroom.

"We saved the best part for last," Summer said excitedly, running to the kitchen and opening a sliding-glass door.

"Wow." Maggie stood on a large deck overlooking an enormous, fenced-in backyard.

"Big enough for a pool," her mom whispered, coming up beside her.

"What's the catch?"

"No catch." Her dad stood on her other side.

"This is in our budget? Something that looks brand-new and doesn't require bulldozing or massive renovating is in our budget?"

"It just came on the market and is reasonably priced because the owner's anxious to sell," her dad explained. "All we have to do is make an offer."

"And it's in your school district," her mom added, putting

one arm across Maggie's shoulder and squeezing. "This is it. This is our house."

"Wow." Maggie looked across the sprawling backyard and smiled slowly as the reality sunk in. "Wow."

"So, we're in agreement?" her dad asked quietly as the realtor came onto the deck from inside.

Maggie and Summer nodded, and Maggie's mom's eyes filled with tears.

"Then let's get our house."

18.

Tucked back from Main Street in a narrow, flower-filled alleyway, The Nook bookstore was Maggie's idea of heaven on earth. Inside, floor-to-ceiling oak shelves were lined with thousands of classic and contemporary books, and worn velvet sofas and chairs invited customers to enjoy hours of uninterrupted reading while soft jazz played overhead. In the back of the store, a "Tea and Crumpets" station sat on an antique beverage cart, and was always well stocked with complimentary hot teas and coffee, and freshly baked cookies, blueberry muffins, and scones. Maggie had easily spent hundreds of hours there, reading, browsing new titles or even studying for school, and it had become the one place—besides the swimming pool—where she always felt completely welcome.

Until now.

Ben had offered to pick her up, but Maggie suggested they just meet at the store. To avoid an unwanted (even if friendly) inquisition, she told her parents she was going to Arnie's to work on the Patrol This website, and rode her bike two miles to town. In her nervous excitement, she'd arrived forty-five minutes early, plopped on a wooden bench in the narrow alleyway, and had yet to venture inside the store that was suddenly not a warm and inviting literary oasis, but a quaint backdrop for potential social disaster.

She checked her watch, and her heart fluttered in her chest when she saw it was six on the dot. The reading started at six-fifteen, and they'd decided to meet a few minutes early to get tea and good seats. She quickly checked her hair in her reflection in the window behind her, applied a fresh coat of lip gloss (even though the last coat couldn't have worn off in the five minutes since its application), and smoothed the front of her long black tank top, which she wore over white capris. (She'd considered wearing a sundress, but didn't want to look like she thought it was a date if it wasn't a date, and also didn't want to give passersby a very embarrassing show while she rode her bike.)

Satisfied her appearance was as good as it was going to get, she rummaged through her purse, counted the roses on the bush next to the bench, and wished she'd brought a book so that she looked busy when Ben approached. When it seemed like an eternity had passed, she checked her watch again. 6:14.

She frowned and felt her cheeks grow warm. Had she misunderstood? Did she have the right store? Did she really tell him not to pick her up at her house? Did he change his mind?

"Madge."

She spun around and willed her eyes dry as they threatened to tear in relief. Ben, looking better than she'd ever seen him in baggy khakis, a white polo shirt, and brown sandals, stood in the doorway of The Nook.

"There you are." He grinned. "I thought you'd changed your mind."

"It was touch-and-go for a while," she joked, smiling and standing from the bench.

"Hope it's okay," he said, holding the door open for her, "but I got here early to grab seats and snacks."

"Great." As she smiled over her shoulder, he held one finger to his lips and nodded toward the back of the store.

Maggie faced forward to see every seat in the house taken, including the fifteen folding chairs set up specifically for the event. The audience talked quietly among themselves as the author, a silver-haired gentleman in a white linen suit and turquoise bifocals, sank into a blue velvet armchair and flipped through a thick book.

"We're in the back," Ben whispered.

Maggie made her way to the only empty sofa, which sat off to the side of the collection of folding chairs. Once seated, they had a perfect, unobstructed view of the entire store, including the author.

"Cookie?" Ben asked softly, lifting a silver platter piled high with an assortment of fresh fruit tarts, chocolate chip cookies, and pound cake from the side of the sofa. "I assembled our own selection from the cart."

Her heart fluttered in her chest. She had absolutely no intention of eating in front of him—especially not anything even with one gram of sugar that might make him wonder as to her past—but he'd assembled their own selection. She couldn't be rude.

"Welcome, everyone," a bookstore employee said before Maggie could respond, "to another exciting installment of the summer author series at The Nook. We're positively honored to have with us today Leonard Hawkins, the multi-award-winning author of more than a dozen novels. Several of Leonard's works have enjoyed lengthy stays on the *New York Times* bestseller list, and even more have been made into major movies. We're very fortunate to have him here to read from his latest novel. Please join me in giving him a warm welcome."

"This is so exciting," Maggie whispered, finally breaking off a piece of pound cake to be polite as the store filled with applause.

She never thought she'd be able to focus on anything but the fact that she was sitting six inches from Ben, who was beautiful and smart and kind, and who'd asked *her* to hang out, but apparently Leonard Hawkins's novels had spent time on the *New York Times* bestseller list for good reason. The excerpt from his latest work, a political mystery set in the year 3000, was so intriguing, Maggie could've been reading the book herself, all alone in an empty room. She spent the entire hour hanging onto every word, and it wasn't until Leonard closed the book that she remembered where she was and that she still held a hunk of pound cake in one hand.

"Not bad, huh?" Ben smiled.

"Unbelievable." Maggie shook her head.

After Ben replaced the platter (with Maggie's uneaten pound cake) on the store's silver snack cart, they joined the exiting crowd and made their way back outside.

"Ben, thank you *so* much," Maggie said as they left the alleyway and neared the stand where she'd locked her bike.

"This was really great. Probably the best night I've had in a long time."

"Throwing in the towel already, Madge?"

She looked at him to see if he was kidding.

"It's still early. I thought we could walk around, maybe grab something to eat."

"Eat? Really?" For some reason, even when she'd briefly let herself believe this might be a date, she'd never imagined it lasting beyond the reading.

"You usually do dinner, yes?"

She nodded and looked to the ground so he couldn't see her growing smile. "Yes."

"Great. There's a phenomenal Thai place around the corner. What do you think?"

"Ben! Maggie!"

They turned around to see Polly hurrying toward them, holding an ice-cream cone in one hand and dragging Jason down the sidewalk with the other.

"Hey, Pols. What're you guys up to?"

"Save me." Jason gasped and grabbed Maggie's arm.

"Shopping." Polly shot Jason a look before letting go of his hand. "No running this time."

"Polly decided I was in major need of . . ." Jason looked at her. "What'd you call it?"

"An overdue wardrobe overhaul," she said proudly, licking her ice-cream cone.

"Right. Which pretty much means dragging me into a million stores, throwing me random clothes that all look exactly the same, and shoving me into dressing room after dressing room."

"Brutal," Ben said sympathetically.

"Hey, no pain, no gain. We girls understand that, don't we, Maggie?"

"Sure."

"Do you think Ben gets home delivery of nice clothes?" Polly turned to Jason. "See how good he looks right now? He had to actually go to a store and try stuff on to look like that."

"You really only have to go once to figure out your sizes and then you can order everything online without ever having to set foot in a store again."

"Thanks a bunch, Ben." Polly sighed.

"Dude. The music store's three doors away. . . ."

"Actually, Maggie and I were just about to grab something to eat."

"That's okay." Maggie smiled and waved one hand. "I'm not starving. We can hit a few stores first."

"Perfect!" Polly grabbed Maggie's hand. "You guys shop for CDs, we'll shop for skirts."

Before she knew it, she and Polly were down the sidewalk, around the corner, and in Stella's, a trendy boutique she'd passed countless times but never set food inside.

"Don't you just love this place?" Polly stopped short just inside the store and picked up a funky brown skirt with suede fringe. "I stop in every week to check out the new shipment."

"I've actually never been here before."

Polly looked at her, eyes wide. "How's that possible?"

Maggie shrugged. The truth was that when she was finally old enough to wear the clothes in the store, she was too heavy and didn't fit in the clothes in the store, but that wouldn't do well as an explanation.

"Don't worry," Polly reassured her, already distracted by a tiny white tunic. "You're here now, and we'll make sure you're initiated appropriately."

As Polly sifted through a rack of shorts that were so short, Maggie'd have to sew three pairs together to make them the length of her regular shorts, Maggie strolled through the store. For a very long time, she'd lived in a boring uniform of jeans and baggy hooded sweatshirts that she got at Lane Bryant or ordered from JCPenney; when she lost enough weight to start wearing clothes from the Gap, J.Crew, and all the other stores at the mall that normal girls shopped in, she'd loaded up on cute skirts, dresses, pants, and T-shirts, all of which kind of looked the same (Jason had a point), and none of which looked anything like the trendy clothes at Stella's. These were a little too loud, a little too wild for Maggie's taste. Plus, the medium she usually wore would probably translate to an extra-large here, and she didn't think she was emotionally prepared for that yet.

"Ready?" Polly stopped short in front of her, embracing a mountain of clothes. "What's the matter? Why are your hands empty?"

"Nothing's the matter. I just don't know if this stuff is really my style."

Polly smiled at her over the top of the mountain. "It's your style. You just don't know it yet." She dashed into a dressing room, unloaded her clothes on the zebra-printed plastic bench, ran back onto the floor, did a thirty-second lap around the store, and came back holding two dresses, three skirts, and two shirts. "Trust me," she said, holding them out to Maggie.

Deciding she had nothing to lose and lots of time to kill since Polly was going to be in there a while, she took the clothes. "Thanks." She entered the dressing room next to Polly's and pulled the magenta satin curtain shut.

As a general rule, dressing rooms still made her uncomfortable. After stretching the curtain as far as it would go so that no one could see in the narrow spaces between its edges and the doorway, she turned away from the full-length mirror. Taking her shirt off but leaving everything else on, she tried on the skirts and T-shirts, turning only briefly to catch her reflection. The clothes fit—which was almost reason enough to buy them—and were sort of cute, but definitely not for her. She didn't even try on the dress, which was super-short, strapless, and tangerine orange.

Back in the store, she sat on a fuzzy black ottoman until Polly came out, carrying the entire mountain in her arms. "No luck?" Maggie asked sympathetically.

"I'm taking it all." Polly looked at Maggie, then at her empty dressing room. "Where's your stuff?"

"Oh, nothing was really right. No biggie."

"What about the orange dress?"

"Nope. Not quite right."

Polly hurried to the front counter, dropped off her new wardrobe, grabbed the orange dress from its rack, and hung it back in Maggie's dressing room. "Just try it again. And let me see."

"You really do take this seriously," Maggie teased.

"Ben will thank me, and you will too. I promise." She smiled and flopped on the ottoman.

Having no choice, Maggie returned to the dressing room. She stretched the curtain, turned away from the mirror, took off her tank top, and pulled the orange dress on over her head. Facing the mirror, she laughed.

"What's so funny?"

Maggie pulled the curtain to one side. "I look like I'm wearing a gum wrapper."

"How can you tell how it looks when you're wearing another entire outfit underneath? Get back in there. Take off the capris."

Maggie did as she was told. Facing the mirror this time, she didn't laugh. The dress definitely wasn't something she'd normally wear—it stopped about four inches too short above the knees for that—but it was definitely something she could imagine someone else her same height, age, and weight wearing.

Polly gasped.

Holding the curtain to one side, Maggie looked down at the dress.

"It's gorgeous. Buy it immediately."

"I don't know," Maggie said doubtfully. "It's not really me."

"Bra straps."

"What?"

"Tuck them into the top of the dress so we get the full effect."

Maggie again did what she was told and stepped out of the dressing room to face the three-way mirror hanging just outside.

"Gorgeous." Polly beamed. "Stunning. Radiant. I knew it."

Maggie inspected her reflection. She had to admit it wasn't as bad as she'd thought. Her arms and legs were tan from spending so much time outside, and her shoulders, toned from swimming, looked great without straps or sleeves. Her dark brown hair, which was also lighter from so much time in the sun, hung in loose waves down her back. "It's just so short."

Polly jumped up from the ottoman and stood by Maggie. "You're young, beautiful, and in great shape. Now's the time to wear stuff like this." She lowered her voice. "See that girl near the register?"

Maggie followed Polly's eyes in the mirror to a twenty-something woman holding the same dress, but in green, against her torso.

"*She* should definitely not wear this dress. In fact, she should be shopping at Lane Bryant or somewhere else that caters to the fuller figured."

As Polly swallowed a giggle, Maggie watched the woman in the mirror. She was much thinner than Maggie'd been at her highest weight. "I'll take it," she said suddenly.

Before she could change her mind, Maggie returned to the dressing room, put on her regular clothes, and headed for the register, heart racing and Camp Sound View earnings and orange dress in hand. She had no idea when or where she'd wear the dress, but the point was that she never would've even considered buying it before. She never would've even considered trying it on before, even despite Polly's best efforts.

And now . . . who knew?

"Okay, I think we have about fifteen minutes before they start serving breakfast."

"We weren't that long," Polly scoffed, swatting Jason with her shopping bags as they rejoined the boys outside.

"Get anything good?" Ben smiled and stood from the bench where he and Jason had been flipping through newly purchased CDs.

"Actually, yes," Maggie said, returning his smile and feeling her cheeks redden, as though she were wearing the short dress right then.

As they followed Jason and Polly into the Thai restaurant, Ben put his hand lightly on Maggie's back, sending a chill greater than any she had felt watching lightning bolts dance before her in the pouring rain up and down her spine.

She didn't know if it was Ben, the dress, or the excitement of the day, but as she sat with her new friends in the dimly lit restaurant, she found herself talking, joking, and laughing much more than usual—so much so, she hardly felt like the same, ordinary Maggie Bean. She felt like someone other people would actually want to know. And the only clue that the old, shy, insecure Maggie was still around was when she ordered steamed chicken and broccoli—no sauce, no rice—while everyone else ordered pad thai.

Now that she was Maggie who owned a cute, short orange dress, there was no way she'd ever be Maggie in jeans and a baggy hooded sweatshirt again. And she didn't want Ben to ever know that that's who she used to be.

19. "Do I have the wrong classroom?" Maggie stepped back to look at the number above the door.

"Why would you ask such a thing?" Electra asked sweetly, dumping the contents of a brown paper grocery bag onto the snack table.

"Kit Kats, Rolos, Snickers, Reese's Peanut Butter Cups, Reese's Pieces, M&M's, Nestlé Crunch, Butterfingers, Baby Ruths, Mounds, Whoppers, Almond Joy, Twix, Dots, gummi bears, gummi worms, Starburst, Skittles, Swedish Fish, and Twizzlers," Maggie said, reading the familiar labels as she neared the snack table. "Am I being punished for something?"

"Don't forget Ding Dongs, Ho Hos, Twinkies, Pop-Tarts, Chips Ahoy!, Oreos, Nutter Butters, and every flavor of Girl Scout cookie." Electra leaned toward Maggie. "The photo slideshow I got. The sugar overdose is still a mystery."

"Arnie," Maggie called across the room, "has Splenda knocked sugar completely out of the junk-food ring?"

"Come see this." He smiled over his laptop screen.

"What's with the trick-or-treat-bag explosion?"

"You'll find out," he said quickly, turning the laptop toward her. "Look."

"'Dear Arnie and Maggie,'" Maggie read. "'Congratulations on your weight-loss success, and thank you for sharing your experience with kids all over the country. Because you care, our children will be healthier and happier. Many thanks, Deb V., Hoboken, New Jersey.'" She looked at him. "Hoboken?"

"It's our very first message on our new message boards," he said, typing quickly. "People can exchange notes on a variety of topics, including everything from fun snack suggestions to favorite movies."

"What's that flashing box at the bottom of the screen?"

Arnie clicked on it, and the box grew to reveal lines of moving text. "Chat room."

Maggie gasped. "Those are real people in there right now?"

"People have been in there since noon. I launched it at eleven forty-five."

"What're they talking about?"

"Mostly where they're from, how old they are, where they go to school. But that's just the beginning. It's what we did with the kids here last week. It's part of building trust, which is so essential to the weight-loss process."

"Arnie," Maggie said, throwing both arms around his shoulders and squeezing, "it's actually working."

"And I played with the layout some more, and added the recipes you e-mailed—which were great, by the way. I already tried the baked whole wheat pita crisps with low-fat spinach dip. Delicious. I also added a few of my favorite songs that make jogging feel less like the torture it really is— Pearl Jam, Coldplay, and Enrique Iglesias."

"You have quite an ear."

"You can add yours, too. And then other people can submit their songs, and we can make a whole Patrol This mix. And maybe even get it on iTunes."

"How long did it take you to do all this?" Maggie asked in awe.

He shrugged. "Not long."

"Right."

"Okay, more than a few hours. But it's fun." He clicked out of the website and closed the laptop.

"Hi, Arnie! Hi, Maggie!"

"Hey there, Lucy Goose!" Arnie held out one hand as Lucy ran at him full-speed. "What're we doing today?" she asked, smacking Arnie's hand so hard with her own, he flinched.

"That's a very good question, Lucy." Maggie smiled.

"Guys," Lucy's mother called, her voice simultaneously confused and concerned, "there's enough sugar here to put a nondiabetic into a coma."

"What *is* with the sweets?" Maggie whispered as Lucy joined her mother and the other arriving kids and parents near the snack table.

"Everything in small doses," he said with a grin—as though that served as an explanation—before standing and addressing the room. "Okay, everyone, we'll get to the candy eventually, I promise. But first we have some boring business stuff to take care of."

Maggie joined him when he leaned against the front edge of the teacher's desk.

"So, how're we doing?" Arnie clapped his palms together. "Good week all around?"

"I went miniature golfing," Paolo announced.

"I saw three movies," Margo added.

Arnie waited patiently for each update. "That's great. Sounds like you're keeping busy and having fun. We're going to have fun today, too. But first, let me run something by you."

Maggie watched the kids and parents watch Arnie curiously.

"You know there are a few things we have to do here—things that if we didn't do, Maggie and I would have no way of knowing if we were helping you the way we should."

"Oh, no," Hannah groaned dramatically.

Arnie laughed. "How do you know what I'm going to say?"

"It's the scale." She shook her head. "I just know it's the scale."

"Okay," Arnie conceded. "It is the scale—"

The room filled with boos and jeers as the rest of the kids echoed Hannah's reaction.

"But I promise it'll be super fast, easy, and pain-free. See that silver curtain over there? It's been scientifically tested for visibility and privacy—no one can see in, and no one can see out. All you'll need to do is hop on, let Maggie fiddle with the bar and talk about how much she hates scales, hop off, and you're done."

"I really do hate scales," Maggie added, hoping the shared sentiment would help the kids feel more comfortable.

"Who doesn't? But we promise that no one but you,

Maggie, and eventually me will know what happens behind that curtain."

"And the parents," Margo's mom reminded him.

"Nope." Arnie shook his head. "Not even the parents. Unless the kids want to share themselves, but that's up to them."

Maggie watched the kids sit quietly in their chairs. They didn't look like they were getting ready to go to Disney World, but they didn't look like they were about to run screaming from the room either.

"So what do we say? Under a minute each, and then it's on to fun stuff?"

"Let's get it over with," Jack said, glancing around at the other kids.

"Great! Love the enthusiasm." Arnie turned, leaned across the desk, and grabbed a plastic bag from the floor by the chair. "Look alive, Jack."

Jack grinned, the looming pain of the scale temporarily eased, when he caught the blue Frisbee.

"That there is a little piece of blue plastic fun, and shameless promotion for our all-new, really cool website."

"'www.PatrolThis.com,'" Jack read from the top of the Frisbee.

"We're going to toss it around outside while everyone

takes turns behind the silver curtain, and later, when you get home and can't stop thinking about just how much fun you had today, you can refer to your very own Frisbee—which you'll receive at the end of the meeting—visit the website, play around, and shoot us an e-mail to tell us what you think."

"Brilliant." Maggie patted Arnie on the back as the kids and parents got up to head outside.

Not only was it an easy way to get kids to exercise and an excellent marketing tool, the Frisbee was also a great distraction. So great that when Maggie asked Hannah if she'd like to go behind the silver curtain first, she dragged her feet because she watched everyone go outside through the door at the back of the classroom, and not because she dreaded getting on the scale.

"Can we make this quick, please?" she asked politely.

"Absolutely." Maggie held up Electra's silver cape for them to duck under.

"Do you really hate scales?" Hannah kicked off her shoes and stepped on to the small platform.

"I really do. I used to hate them more than anything, but now I know they're meant for good, not evil." Maggie waited for the scale's bar to stop moving, and adjusted the weights.

"Is Arnie your boyfriend?"

Maggie laughed.

"He's cute. And funny."

Watching the bar balance, Maggie nodded. "He is definitely both of those things."

"So is he?" Hannah looked at her and smiled, as though she knew something Maggie didn't. "Your boyfriend?"

"Nope, we're just friends. Really good friends. Best friends, in fact." She wasn't sure why she felt the need to clarify so thoroughly, but she guessed it had something to do with the way Ben's face sprang to mind at the term "boyfriend."

"I hope I have a boyfriend someday." Hannah glanced quickly at the metal bar before looking down and sighing.

"You will. I promise," Maggie said gently, knowing the feeling all too well. She confirmed Hannah's weight, marked it on the yellow piece of construction paper (less intimidating than a clipboard, but just as effective), and slid the square weights back to the end of the metal bar. "Okay, all set. Do you want to know what the scale said?"

Hannah hopped off, put on her shoes, and looked at Maggie like she was joking.

"Got it." Maggie grinned and held up the silver cape for Hannah to duck under. "Great job. Can you send in Margo, please?"

As Maggie continued the weigh-in, she noticed each kid seemed happier—and sweatier—than the one before. They were so excited to get back outside, it was all they could do to stand still long enough for the metal bar to adjust and Maggie to write down the number. When she'd recorded the very last weight, she emerged from the makeshift silver tent, carefully tucked the construction paper in a folder, put the folder in Arnie's backpack (so there was no chance of accidental information sharing), and headed for the door at the back of the classroom.

Arnie and the kids ran around the large courtyard, tossing, catching, and dropping the Frisbee. The parents stood at the edge of the lawn, talking and shaking their heads in wonder. Maggie guessed it was probably the first time they'd seen their children exercise in a very long time.

"Okay!" Arnie caught the Frisbee and held on to it when he spotted Maggie in the doorway. "That was awesome. Let's slow down, catch our breaths, and head back in."

"Pure genius," Maggie whispered to Arnie as everyone filed into the classroom.

He ruffled her hair and grabbed two cups of water from the snack table. "So," he said after they'd reached the teacher's desk and everyone else had taken their seats and quieted down. "Who likes candy? Cookies? Cake?"

When the kids exchanged confused looks, silently asking one another if it was a trick question, Maggie shot one arm in the air. "Reese's Pieces. Candy-coated peanut-butter pellets of bliss."

"I'm an Almond Joy fan, myself," Arnie admitted, raising his hand. "Coconut, almonds—it's like a chocolaty tropical vacation."

"I like Snickers, but my parents said I shouldn't eat them," Alex said, and pouted at his mom.

"Well, why don't you all head over to the snack table and pick out your favorite treat—the one thing you dream of when you want something sweet."

The kids stood uncertainly from their chairs and headed for the snack table. Five seconds later, they were much more relaxed as they sifted through the extensive selection and made their picks.

"Great choices," Arnie said when the kids returned to their seats. "Now, here's what I want you to think about. Alex's parents are right: There are much better, healthier snack choices out there than chocolate and cookies. But everything—even Snickers, Almond Joys, and Reese's Pieces—is okay once in a while. The trick is to not eat two candy bars every day, but maybe one every week. So, I want you to take that candy home with you today and see if you can hold on to it until our meeting next week. If you can, and if you still want it by then, we'll all eat together."

They spent the rest of the meeting talking about all their favorite foods, and why sometimes they craved pizza, and other times ice-cream sundaes. After a while, even the parents—who had seemed initially unhappy with the introduction of candy—chimed in with their favorite pasta dishes and accompanying wines (a tangent Arnie brought back to kid-friendly by talking about his love of Dr Pepper). They talked until it was time to go, and then a few minutes past then, since no one seemed in an especially big hurry to leave. When the classroom was finally empty, Maggie and Arnie flopped into two desk chairs, simultaneously exhilarated and exhausted.

"Have I told you how amazing you are?" Maggie shook her head. "Frisbees, candy, the website . . . soon every kid in the neighborhood is going to want to join our little club, even if they don't have any weight to lose."

"It's a team effort. We're a team."

"But you're doing most of the work. What can I do to help?"

"We'll talk about it when we plan next week. To start, you can always add your photo slideshow and story to the website."

"Sorry." Maggie winced. "I know I was supposed to do that." She'd promised him last week that she'd have it done for this week. But that was before her life had taken a slight, unexpected detour.

"It's no big deal. But it'd be great for little girls to have a mature woman's perspective." He grinned.

"I know. And I'll get the pictures, I promise."

He tilted back in his chair and put his hands behind his head. "We should celebrate."

"Celebrate?"

"You and me. We should go out on the boat."

"Sure. That'd be great."

"How about this weekend?"

Maggie paused. She'd already made plans to see a movie with Ben, Polly, and Jason on Friday, and to go shopping with Polly on Saturday. "I'm kind of busy this weekend."

"Oh. Okay. How about the weekend after that?"

She chewed her lip. She didn't have plans for the weekend after that, but wanted to keep it open, just in case. "Can we talk about it next week? I'm just not sure what my schedule's like."

He nodded. "Of course."

Not sure why she was suddenly nervous, Maggie jumped from the chair and started collecting the leftover candy.

It wasn't that she didn't want to tell Arnie about her new friends (she knew he'd be happy that the job was working out so well); she just didn't feel like answering any questions the topic might bring. Besides, her life with Arnie was entirely separate from her life with Ben, Polly, and Jason. And right now, she wanted to keep it that way.

20.

Maggie's arms cut through the cool water quickly and easily, and her legs propelled her forward almost automatically. Her breathing was steady as she finished a ninth lap, then a tenth. Swimming in the lake was definitely different from swimming in the chlorinated school pool (for many reasons, not the least of which being the slimy, stringy seaweed that grabbed at her limbs and the small schools of fish that flitted around her), but there was one thing that would always be the same, no matter where she swam: In the water, she was a stronger person.

It had been true from the first time Aimee forced her into the pool before Water Wings tryouts. Maggie, then deathly terrified of being seen in her bathing suit in public, had found sweet relief in simply shielding her body from curious onlookers by getting in the water; the feeling was quickly replaced by intense exhilaration as she forgot about her embarrassment and actually attempted the crawl, then the backstroke, sidestroke, and every other stroke she could think of. That rush of energy had only grown when she joined the school swim tea m months later, and daily practices improved her technique, making her strokes crisper and kicks sharper. Now, just like anytime she'd been in water in the past year, the hardest part about swimming was stopping.

It almost didn't even matter that a boy waited for her on the beach.

"Hey, Ariel!"

Maggie finished an eleventh lap before slowing down and allowing her arms and legs to tread gently in the water. She looked toward shore, where Ben and Jason had already completed their beach sprints.

"The rug rats, including Erin, will be here soon, and your breakfast's getting cold." Ben lifted the brown paper bag that sat on the sand between him and Jason. "Even little mermaids need fuel to get through the day."

She grinned and paddled toward the beach. These morning workouts, which she'd been joining Ben and Jason for two or three times a week, had quickly become her favorite time of the day—besides when she hung out with Ben, Jason, Polly, and occasionally some of the other camp counselors after work, which had somehow become a regular occurrence over the past two weeks. She still wasn't clear on whether Ben liked her as anything more than a friend—invitations to hang out at Polly's, go to the movies, mini-golf, and shop were always thrown out casually, usually when they were cleaning the beach at the end of the day—but she was so thrilled to be included, she didn't try too hard to figure it out.

"Sorry." She hurried out of the water, wrapped her towel around her waist, and flopped on the sand. "Cold fruit salad is the worst."

"You eat like a bird," Jason said, tossing her the plastic container and fork. "Why do girls do that?"

"I do *not* eat like a bird."

"Yes, you do. I practically pass out on the beach after swimming every morning and long for a respirator as my weak muscles quiver and shake. I *need* three bagels, four bananas, three oranges, and two Yoo-Hoos to keep going. You swim twenty miles, jog out of the water as easily as if you'd been sunning on a raft, eat a handful of grapes and strawberry slices, and are ready to go." Jason shoved half a cinnamon-raisin bagel with cream cheese in his mouth. "I'm so glad I'm not a girl."

Maggie's stomach grumbled quietly as she opened the fruit salad container. She was eating like a bird, it was true. If she'd been by herself after swimming like that, she'd devour granola, oatmeal, or whole wheat toast with peanut butter to satisfy her hard-earned hunger. But even though she knew no one would even notice, let alone have a clue as to her chocolate-coated past, she always requested the same small fruit salad when Ben asked for requests for the next day's deli run.

"We should go to Danger Nation this weekend."

Maggie silently thanked Ben for the subject change.

"Life-threatening roller coasters, ten-dollar hot dogs." Jason nodded. "I'm there."

"You in, Madge?" Ben elbowed her gently. "Saturday?"

"I don't think I can," she said reluctantly. She'd love nothing more than the chance to get stuck at the very top of an enormous Ferris wheel with Ben—such fear-inducing, adrenaline-pumping moments always brought people closer—but amusement park visits were all-day affairs. And there was no way she could miss the weekly Patrol This meeting, especially since she'd been there in body but barely in mind the past few weeks. Arnie hadn't noticed—or, if he had, he'd kept it to himself—but she still felt guilty.

"But who will hold my hand on the scary rides?" Jason pouted. "And win me stuffed animals?"

"Sorry, guys. I wish I could, believe me."

"Isn't this cute."

They turned around to see Erin standing behind them, arms crossed over her chest.

"Don't mean to interrupt your little tea party—"

"Yes, you do."

"But you might want to clean up this mess before the campers arrive in about thirty seconds." She scowled at Jason.

Not one to ignore authority figures—even cranky, unreasonable ones—Maggie jumped up, collected their empty wrappers and containers in the brown paper bag, and headed for the garbage can by the lifeguard stand.

"Nice hustle, Bean," Erin said sarcastically.

"Bright and sunny as usual," Maggie commented when Ben stood beside her.

"Erin's bed has no right side to wake up on in the morning." He finished eating an apple and tossed the core into the trash.

"Why not?"

Ben leaned closer to her. "She kind of doesn't have many friends. And she really hates that we're all friends with each other."

"Oh." Before she could ask why, or whether anyone had ever tried inviting her to join in an after-work activity, Ben grabbed her hand and led her gently down the beach.

"What're you doing? Where are we going?" Maggie glanced over her shoulder. "The campers really will be here any minute."

He quickened his pace and pulled her gently behind a beach boulder where no one could see them but the seagulls flying overhead. He shrugged his backpack from his shoulders, opened it, and pulled out a book.

"Leonard Hawkins, cool." Maggie immediately recognized the silver-haired author in turquoise bifocals from the reading on the back cover. "Did you finish it? Any good?"

"You ask a lot of questions, Madge." He smiled and handed her the book. "Open it."

Turning to the title page, Maggie gasped. "'Dear Maggie. Happy reading. With best wishes, Leonard Hawkins.'"

"Do you like it?"

"When did you, how did you . . . ?" She trailed off and stared at the small, neat handwriting.

"I dragged Jason back to The Nook when Polly dragged you to Stella's."

She looked at him. "For me?"

He laughed. "Yes, for you."

"Well, thank you." She shook her head and looked back at the inscription. "So much. I love it."

She held her breath when he suddenly took a step closer.

"I had a great time with you that night, Madge. I *have* a great time with you, whenever we hang out. And I just wanted you to know."

Before Maggie could ignore her pounding heart long enough to raise her eyes to meet his, he gently pushed her damp hair away from her face, leaned forward, and kissed her cheek.

"Come to Danger Nation Saturday," he said softly, his face still close to hers.

A thousand thoughts shot through her head—the Patrol This meeting, letting Arnie down, the fact that a boy had just kissed her (on the cheek, but still undeniable lip-to-skin contact), the fact that said boy was still so close, she could smell lake water and sunscreen—but only one word made it through her mouth. "Okay."

Three piercing whistles sounded suddenly down the beach, saving Maggie from struggling to say something else wittier and more charming.

"Erin has spoken." Grinning, Ben zipped his backpack and slung it on one shoulder. "Ready?"

She had no idea *what* she was ready for right at that moment, but she clutched the book to her chest and managed to follow him back toward the lifeguard stand and the arriving campers.

"We'll talk more later," he said when a dozen excited Freshwater Phantoms made a run for him.

Maggie took advantage of the controlled chaos to return to the lifeguard stand and put the book in her backpack. Crouching down, she fiddled with the zipper longer than necessary to give her swirling head a chance to calm down so that it didn't throw off her equilibrium and make her fall over when she tried to stand up. She thought she might have to squat there all day until she spotted her one saving grace walking across the sand.

Aimee.

Her head instantly clear, Maggie jumped up and hurried toward her best friend. They hadn't really spoken since the disastrous phone call two weeks before (Maggie had left several unreturned messages, and they were both so busy at camp, they only managed to wave across crowds of people), but surely they could steal a few minutes to talk now. Maggie had just had her almost-first kiss, after all, and it was pretty much the rule of teenage girlhood that such momentous life-changing news be shared with the best friend first.

"Hi, your royal highness," Maggie said brightly, stopping just behind the Figure Eights. When Aimee didn't turn around right away, Maggie tapped her on the shoulder.

"Oh," Aimee said. "Hey."

"How are you?"

"Fine."

Maggie paused. Technically, they were speaking, but Aimee wasn't smiling and hardly looked at her. "So, I see you're Queen of the Day." She nodded to the silver plastic tiara surrounding the top of Aimee's blond ponytail.

"Queen of the Week, actually. Maybe even the rest of the summer."

"Wow, impressive reign. Congratulations." When Aimee turned slightly as though preparing to return to the group, Maggie touched her arm. "Can we talk for a minute? Alone?"

"There are a hundred people on the beach."

"We'll talk quietly."

"Don't you have to get back to work? Don't the other swim instructors need you?"

"Aimee," Maggie said gently. "Please?"

Aimee's face softened slightly. She whispered something to another Figure Eight, who looked at Maggie suspiciously, then led Maggie ten feet away from the crowd.

"I feel like we haven't really talked in forever."

"That's because we haven't."

"Well, can we stop the silliness?" Maggie asked hopefully. "Starting now?"

Aimee looked down at her bare feet, then up at Maggie. "Sure," she said, almost smiling.

"Thank goodness." Maggie sighed and gave Aimee a quick hug. "I have *so* much to tell you. You won't believe what just happened, like, five minutes ago. Ben and I were hanging out by the lifeguard stand, not talking about much, and then all of a sudden he—"

"Stop."

Maggie stopped. "What's wrong?"

"I can't talk about this." Aimee shook her head and shuffled back toward the Figure Eights.

"Aim, wait." As Maggie ran after her, she was struck by what probably should've been a very obvious thought. She caught up and grabbed Aimee's hand. "Do *you* like Ben? Is that it?"

Aimee's mouth fell open and she stared at Maggie like Maggie had three eyes. Maggie gently let go of Aimee's hand and watched her march back to her group.

Apparently, that wasn't it. Which meant that Maggie had no idea why her best friend in the whole world, the person who usually knew her better than she knew herself, didn't want to talk to her.

21.

"I'm late!" Maggie threw open the front door, grabbed the stuffed lion, elephant, bear, flower, hedgehog, and spider she'd dropped on the stoop to free her hands, and kicked the door shut. "I'm *so* late, but I'm here now and will be ready to go in five minutes."

"Maggie—"

"I know!" Holding the Danger Nation carnival game prizes in front of her face to avoid eye contact with her mom, she sprinted through the living room and down the hall to her room. "Five minutes, I promise!"

She deposited Ben's winnings on her bed and flew to her closet. As she riffled through her clothes, she quickly dismissed every skirt and dress as too boring and plain, and chided herself for not planning ahead. Tonight was a big deal. While she was screaming on roller coasters, watching

Ben and Jason compete at ring toss and other manly games and having one of the best days of her life, her parents had completed all the paperwork and everything needed to make the small white ranch house their new home. To celebrate, they were having a family dinner at Nora's, the nicest restaurant in town, and then going to Home Depot for a paint-shopping extravaganza. A few weeks ago, when she wasn't so busy, Maggie would've carefully considered and chosen her outfit days in advance.

When nothing seemed quite right, Maggie stopped riffling, sighed, and stared at the contents of her closet. Knowing her five minutes were dwindling, she reached for a pair of white pants; as she pulled them from a hanger, a heavy bundle of gray cotton tumbled from the top shelf and fell to the floor.

Maggie eyed the hooded sweatshirt warily. Once upon a time, as the biggest top she'd owned and the easiest to hide in, it had been her favorite wardrobe piece. Seeing it now made her stomach turn, so she kicked it back in the closet, onto a pile of old sneakers and slippers. Her decision suddenly made, she rehung the white pants and grabbed the sleeveless orange dress from Stella's that hung from the top of the closet door. She hadn't worn it since the night she bought it (though she'd spent at least a few minutes each morning and night staring at it and smiling), and had wondered if she'd ever wear it again, since no occasion seemed quite appropriate. She didn't know if a family celebration quite qualified as appropriate, but then, who was to say it didn't?

She quickly shed her shorts and T-shirt and pulled the orange dress over her head. She brushed her hair, put on lip gloss, and finished the entire look with silver flop-flops. Ready to go, she glanced at her dresser mirror to confirm everything was where it should be, and headed for the door.

And then went back to the mirror.

In a "Which of these doesn't belong?" moment, she'd spotted something green, square, and familiar in the mirror's reflection. She leaned toward the mirror for a closer inspection, then turned to the bed.

Maggie pushed aside the mountain of stuffed animals to reveal Arnie's green laptop bag. Inside was his prized MacBook that he never went anywhere without, and a note.

Since you weren't at the meeting today and since I haven't heard from you much lately, I thought I'd make things easier for you. Your slideshow is ready to go, except for captions. Please fill them in so I can post everything to the site. If you changed your mind about the slideshow, or if you don't feel like writing captions, let me know. Also,

if you changed your mind about participating in Patrol
This in general, let me know that, too. Talk soon.

Frowning, Maggie read the note a second, and then a third time. She'd e-mailed Arnie that morning to say something had come up and that she couldn't make the meeting. She hadn't assumed missing one meeting would make it seem like she wanted out entirely, which meant she must've seemed really out of it in recent weeks.

But like most things these days, she didn't have time to worry about that now. She shoved the note back in the bag, zipped the bag, and hurried from the room.

"I'm ready!" Maggie announced brightly, entering the living room. "And *starving*. Bring on Nora's famous chicken parmigiana and—"

"Maggie."

Maggie turned to her mom, who was sitting on the couch with one arm around Summer.

"Wow," Summer said, her eyes traveling from above Maggie's knees to her shoulders.

"Is that new?" Her mom asked, trying not to sound surprised—or alarmed, it was hard to tell which. "The dress?"

"Maggie," her dad said before she could respond, apparently wanting to keep everyone focused. "You knew we had plans to—"

"I'm late, I know. I'm never late, and today was definitely the wrong day to start. It won't happen again."

Her mother looked at her father, who was sitting in an armchair. Summer looked down at her hands in her lap.

"I'm not *that* late," Maggie said meekly.

"Maggie," her father said gently. "There's been a change of plans."

"What do you mean? Are we going to Applebee's instead of Nora's?" It might not have been the best time to attempt a joke, but they all looked so serious, she couldn't help it.

"Why don't you sit?" Her mother patted the couch.

Maggie sat, growing concern replacing the guilt she felt for being late.

"You know we were supposed to finish up the house paperwork today." Her dad leaned forward, rested his elbows on his knees, and clasped his hands.

"Supposed to," Maggie repeated. "Was there a scheduling conflict? Are we postponing the celebration until next week?"

"We're definitely postponing." Her mother sighed.

"So, that's okay," Maggie said brightly. "What's another couple of days after waiting so long?"

"Well, it might be more than a few days," her dad admitted.

"It's hard to tell just how long it will be," her mother added.

"No problem. That'll just give us more time to decide how to make the little white ranch an interior designer's dream."

"The thing is, Maggie . . ." Her mother's voice trailed off.

"Our mortgage fell through," her dad finished.

"Oh." Maggie paused. "What does that mean, exactly?"

"It means the bank won't loan us the money we need to buy the house."

"But I thought it was affordable. I thought that wasn't a question."

"We didn't think it was either," her mom said. "But there are so many little loopholes and ways for these things to not work out."

Maggie shook her head. She hadn't seen them much lately, but she knew her family had been floating on air since they'd looked at the little white ranch. Every time she passed by Summer's room she spotted a new cardboard box filled to the brim, and the dining room table, living room coffee table, kitchen counter, and any available flat surface were covered in her parents' lists and notes about movers, painters, and landscapers. Every sign had indicated that this was a done

Tricia Rayburn

258

deal. "Isn't there any way we change the bank's mind?"

"The only way is to take out a smaller loan," her mother said.

"And the only way we can take out a smaller loan is if we put down a bigger cash deposit on the house," her dad explained.

"So let's do that," Maggie said simply.

"We don't have the money, sweetie." Her mother frowned.

"Well, why don't we just wait a little while until we can save enough money?" Maggie asked logically. Surely this wasn't the big deal they were making it out to be.

"We can try to save more money," her dad said, "and we will. But by the time we save what we need, the little white ranch will be gone."

"It's a great price, and someone else will buy it immediately."

"Some other little girl is going to live in my room," Summer said sadly.

Maggie sat back on the couch, trying to process this information.

"We've talked to everyone there is to talk to about this," her dad said. "We've explored all of our options and imagined every possible financial scenario."

"It just wasn't meant to be," her mother concluded.

"And we're so sorry," her dad added. "We know how excited you and Summer were, and we hate letting you down."

Maggie stared at the hem of her orange dress as one emotion led to the next—confusion, disbelief, disappointment, sadness and, eventually, annoyance. Suddenly unable to sit there one second longer, she jumped up from the couch.

"Maggie?" Her mother's voice was concerned.

"I have to go." Ignoring her parents' surprised looks, she ran to her room, closed the door, and flopped next to the pile of stuffed animals still on her bed.

She knew it wasn't her parents' fault. It probably wasn't even the bank's fault, since there were most likely certain rules that had to be followed, and whoever had turned them down was just doing his or her job. Still, that didn't make it *fair*. And she was pretty tired of things never working out for her the way they always seemed to for other people.

She grabbed the cordless phone from her nightstand. Holding one finger above the number pad, she paused only briefly before dialing Ben's cell phone number. Since they saw each other almost every day, she didn't use it much, but had memorized it about two minutes after he gave it to her.

"Ben?" She strained to hear his voice through static and

what sounded like a lot of people talking and laughing. "It's Maggie."

"Hang on, Madge."

She stared at the peeling paint on the ceiling and listened to the background noise grow quieter.

"Sorry about that. I'm in a different room now."

"No problem. Where are you?"

"Polly's house. She decided to have everyone over for movies and snacks. What's up?"

"Nothing," she said, feeling a combination of jealous and silly for calling as she pictured everyone having fun without her. "I just wanted to say hi."

"Hi. Why aren't you with the fam? Isn't tonight the big celebration?"

"It kind of got postponed." Maggie's eyes filled unexpectedly with tears. "The deal fell through."

"Bummer."

"Yeah." She opened her mouth to elaborate, but nothing came out.

"So . . ." He paused. "You're okay, right?"

"Yup." She wiped her eyes with a stuffed elephant. "Just wanted to say hi."

"Okay. Hi," he said again. "Well, I should probably get back to the gang."

"Right." She sniffed. "Have fun."

"You too. See you Monday."

She hung up and rested the phone on her chest. *You too?* Had he even heard what she said? True, he didn't know her family's history, so there was no way he could really know just how big a deal this was, but at the very least, he knew she'd been excited. He knew this was important to her.

She picked up the phone again and started punching the phone number she'd dialed a million times over the past few years. When she was about to hit the seventh number, she stopped. Aimee would know what was up as soon as Maggie said hello, but for whatever reason, they still weren't speaking. Hanging up, she quickly ruled out calling Arnie since his MacBook in her room was a clear indication that he probably wouldn't be up for chatting.

With no one else to call and nowhere to go, Maggie brought her knees to her chest and wrapped her arms around the stuffed lion, elephant, bear, flower, hedgehog, and spider. As she pulled the comforter over her head and waited for sleep to come, for the first time in a very long time, she found herself thinking of chocolate.

22. "Wow." Polly circled Maggie, inspecting her appearance from head to toe and picking off imaginary pieces of lint. "Stunning. You *have* to have it."

Maggie had thought the short black dress with white stripes and sequined hem would make her look like a very trendy, chubby prisoner, but the longer she looked in the full-length mirror, the more it grew on her.

"The v-neck is *amazing* with your haircut."

"Thanks." Maggie smiled. Her new chin-length bob and fringy bangs—which she'd just had done an hour before—did make her neck look longer and thinner. "But do I really need it?"

Polly eyed the mountain of pants, skirts, shorts, shirts, and shoes on top of the zebra-patterned ottoman. "Why stop now?"

"Good point." She ducked back in the dressing room and pulled the magenta satin curtain shut.

"I'm so glad you decided to do this," Polly called through the curtain.

"Me too." As Maggie changed back into her jeans and tank top, she thought about just how true that was. The idea had hit her unexpectedly the day before. She'd been lying in bed, doing her best to avoid any familial interaction (just as she had since the announcement about the mortgage), and had just swapped *Ethan Frome* for *InStyle*. Flipping through the fashion magazine, she'd felt the subtle jealous pangs she usually felt when looking at perfect models and celebrities with perfect bodies, clothes, and hair, and immediately had decided a completely new look was just what she needed. The next day she asked Polly if she'd be up for a shopping spree, and there they were, less than twenty-four hours later.

"Maggie, by the way, what's the deal with the computer?"

"What computer?"

"The one you've been carrying around all day?"

Maggie thought quickly. She'd brought Arnie's MacBook with her just in case she didn't have time to go home before the Patrol This meeting later that afternoon, and hoped if

Polly noticed she would just think it was a new, cool messenger bag. Because why else would she be toting around a laptop while shopping in the middle of a summer afternoon?

"It's a friend's," she said finally, opening the curtain and smiling. "All set."

"You're taking *everything*?" Polly peeked past her at the empty dressing room.

"Why not?"

"You're my hero."

Maggie grabbed the laptop bag from the floor by the ottoman, slung it across her shoulder, and followed Polly to the register. They deposited two piles of clothes next to the two already sitting on the counter. As the saleswoman rang up each item, Polly tried on sunglasses and Maggie watched the green number grow on the register screen.

"Six hundred seventy-three dollars and forty-five cents."

Maggie swallowed. She wanted to look like she did this kind of thing all the time, but of course, she'd never done anything like this—ever. The most expensive thing she'd ever bought (before the sleeveless orange dress) was a pair of Banana Republic jeans, which had cost ninety-eight dollars, and which had prevented her from buying anything else for three months. On top of which, it wasn't like she or her family had the kind of money for such extravagant shopping sprees; in fact, she was pretty sure her mother didn't spend that much money outfitting all four of them in an entire year.

But after losing the little white ranch house, she was *really* tired of worrying about money. And about being good, and responsible, and doing the right thing. Quickly deciding that she was only allowing herself a few minutes of the kind of selfishness every other teenager in America felt entitled to on a daily basis, she calmly opened her purse, took out her wallet, and handed the saleswoman a credit card.

"Parents are the best," Polly said generously.

"Definitely." Except that this was her emergency-only credit card, which she would need again once her parents saw the bill and she was forced to flee the country.

She signed the receipt, took the shiny magenta bags, and felt guiltier than she had in her entire life as they left the store. Fortunately, Ben and Jason waited for them on a bench outside; seeing Ben smile always made it easy to forget everything else and think only of Ben.

"New York City," Jason announced as they neared the bench.

"San Francisco," Polly shot back.

"Next weekend," Jason said. "We'll get a ton of people to go."

"New York's three hours away," Maggie said, as though that were the only reason the idea was completely ridiculous.

"By car. Forty minutes by plane." Ben grinned.

"My dad has a great loft downtown. If I tell him we're coming, he'll make sure the place is stocked and he'll leave money for cabs. All we have to do is pay for the flight and we're set for forty-eight hours of nonstop urban adventure."

"I can't really swing a flight." Glowing green numbers flashed through Maggie's head.

"I'll charge them," Jason said simply. "You all can pay me back whenever."

Suddenly forgetting whether the saleswoman had given back her credit card, Maggie dropped the laptop and shopping bags. She rummaged through her purse for her wallet. "Be right back." She walked away without looking up.

The saleswoman was busy helping a group of girls when Maggie reentered the store. She waited near the register, tapping her fingers on the counter and resisting the urge to climb over it and search. When the saleswoman disappeared in the back to retrieve different sizes of gold high-heeled sandals for the girls, Maggie flipped through the guest book, looked at the store catalog, and considered trying on more clothes (even though she was pretty sure there wasn't anything there she hadn't already tried on) to kill time.

"Can I help you?" the saleswoman finally asked, twenty minutes later.

Nearly dropping the handful of lip-gloss tubes she'd been counting, Maggie turned to the saleswoman. "I think I left my credit card." She shoved the lip gloss tubes back into their plastic display case.

"You did." The saleswoman opened the register, pulled out Maggie's card, and handed it to her. "These aren't toys, you know."

"I know," Maggie said sheepishly. She took the card and put it in her wallet. "Sorry. Thank you."

"Our return policy is thirty days with your receipt for a full refund, store credit after that."

Maggie looked down and nodded. She had a few weeks before her parents found out about this—she'd have to practice being a more convincing charger before then.

Reminding herself it would all be worth it once the old, boring clothes in her closet were replaced by her new, trendy purchases, Maggie hurried from the store. The closet reminder was so effective, she almost didn't think anything of seeing Ben, Jason, and Polly huddled around a glowing laptop screen as she neared the bench.

"Christmas, sixth grade. The year Santa had a better shot of fitting down the chimney. 167 pounds."

"Birthday, sixth grade. I got books, CDs, and DVDs, but breaking the candy-filled piñata open was my favorite present. 170 pounds."

"First day of school, seventh grade. Big book bag, bigger butt. 175 pounds."

Maggie's knees started to tremble, then buckle as Ben, Jason, and Polly pointed, giggled, and took turns reading from the laptop screen. In a desperate attempt to keep Arnie from hating her forever, she'd stayed up late the night before writing captions for her photo slideshow. She must've left it up on the screen after saving the changes.

"Oh, wow. I had no idea pizza could make one person so happy." Jason shook his head.

Maggie forced her legs to move before she worsened the new Most Embarrassing Moment Ever by collapsing to the sidewalk. Ducking behind a garbage can, she clutched her purse to her chest, as though the pressure could slow her hammering heart. She knew there was a risk that people she knew would eventually see the Patrol This website—though she and Arnie had agreed on no last names, to protect the innocent—but the risk was never to have presented itself so soon. The photos weren't even on the website yet; she'd assembled the slideshow more for Arnie than for future Patrol This participants.

And the shock of exposure was only magnified exponentially by the fact that here it was again: her old, inescapable self. She'd worked so hard for so long to lose weight and be the kind of person people liked and thought of as more than a smart girl who might *also* be a pretty girl if she only had more self-control in the kitchen. She ate right, got good grades, was an excellent swimmer and, up until recently, was a great friend, sister, and daughter. She did everything she was supposed to do.

So why did this keep happening?

As they continued to whisper and giggle, Maggie frantically weighed her options. She could not go back and hope someone would at least be nice enough to take the laptop and her shopping bags home so she could get them later. She could summon the courage of her most confident, assured, imaginary self, and saunter up, nonchalantly ask what they were looking at, and brush it off as no big deal—something she just forgot to mention. Or, she could try to save them all—including herself—from forced politeness and painfully fake social propriety.

For better or worse, in this situation of fight or flight, there was no fighting the flight.

Maggie peeked around the garbage can to make sure they were still distracted. When Polly said something about Snickers and Jason snorted, Maggie stood, sprinted to Stella's, and went in, and came back out again. "Thank you *so* much," she yelled into the store as she held the door open. "That was really *so* great of you to hold my credit card for me. Does the Better Business Bureau give awards to exceptional employees? Because if they do, I'm calling them right now to nominate you! And if they don't, I'm calling them right now to propose they start, and *then* I'll nominate you. Do you like coffee? Ice cream? Next time I stop in, I'll bring you both!"

Once satisfied she'd given Ben, Jason, and Polly enough time to hide the evidence (and the staff at Stella's enough reason to lock the door if ever she came back, which she now doubted she ever would), Maggie turned and started walking casually toward the bench. "Hey, guys," she said brightly. "I have good news and bad news. The good news is, they had my credit card. The bad news is, I *just* remembered I have a very important thing I should've been at five minutes ago, so I have to run."

Ben swigged from a water bottle, Polly inspected her face in an open compact, and Jason talked on his cell phone. They all sat on the bench just as she'd left them. The laptop was back in its bag, which was back on the ground, next to her shopping bags.

"Are you sure you have to go?" Ben asked, looking in her direction, but not quite at her.

"Yup." Deciding there was no way she could look any of them in the eye herself, she grabbed the three shopping bags and laptop bag.

"That's too bad," Polly said, pouting into the compact mirror. "We were having *such* a great day."

"I know. We'll do it again soon." She winced slightly at the hopefulness in her voice. She should've been so infuriated that the idea of spending even five more seconds with any of them would send her running in the other direction. And she *was* infuriated—but she was also sad.

The conflicting emotions were too much to process right then, so Maggie smiled, waved, and hurried down the sidewalk toward her bike, which she'd locked, very unfortunately, near The Nook. Careful not to look down the small alley leading to the bookstore, she climbed on the bike and balanced the weight of all her bags on both shoulders. She peddled slowly at first, unsure of whether it was the extra baggage she carried or the tornado of thoughts in her head that made her unsteady. Once she could ride in a straight line, she pushed her legs to gain momentum. Soon she was flying down the street as her shiny magenta shopping bags flapped against her back and tears streamed from the far corners of her eyes, toward her ears. And she would've flown all the way home, bags flying and tears streaming, except for one previously unplanned stop.

The drugstore candy aisle.

23.

"Well, good heavens. When'd the hurricane hit?"

Maggie opened her eyes under the comforter.

"Was it during *Deal or No Deal*? I am so ga-ga over that Howie Mandel, my house could get swept up, spun about, and dropped in another county during his show and I'd have no idea."

Maggie held her breath. Maybe if she didn't move, Aunt Violetta would mistake the blanketed bulge for pillows and crumpled sheets and go away.

Aunt Violetta sat on the edge of Maggie's bed. "Hiya, kiddo." She patted Maggie's covered head.

Maggie sighed. There was no use even trying. She could ignore her parents—a skill she'd perfected the last two weeks—but Aunt Violetta was another story. Maggie knew it, Aunt Violetta knew it, and her parents certainly knew it, which had to explain the surprise visit. They'd called in reinforcements.

"What do we have here?"

Maggie listened to the crinkling of plastic.

"Kit Kats, yum."

"Aunt Violetta," Maggie said from underneath the blanket. "It's really nice to see you, but I'm very busy."

"Oh?"

"Yes. And I don't feel well."

"That's tough. It's always hard to be busy when you're sick." She clucked her tongue.

"I knew you'd understand. So if you don't mind . . ."

"I don't mind a bit. I have an impenetrable immune system."

Maggie grabbed the top of the blanket and lowered it just enough to see into her room.

"Is this the first time you're seeing the storm's damage?"

Maggie watched Aunt Violetta look around her room and shake her head sadly, as though a hurricane really had blown through. Not that it didn't look like it—clothes, books, papers, magazines, and tissues littered the floor, bed, desk, and dresser. Scattered among all that were full bags, half-full bags, and empty bags of Kit Kats, Snickers,

M&M's, Reese's Pieces, Rolos, Milky Ways, Reese's Peanut Butter Cups, Hershey Kisses, Three Musketeers, and Twix. And scattered amongst all *that* were dozens of silver, gold, black, and brown wrappers. None of which was that bad, though, at least not compared to the room's southeast corner, into which she'd flung the stuffed lion, elephant, bear, flower, hedgehog, and spider from Danger Nation, and the three magenta shopping bags from Stella's, still filled with clothes she'd never wear.

"So, should we start with what you know, or what I know?"

Maggie rolled onto her side, away from Aunt Violetta and toward the wall.

"I do love to go first. Okay, I'll give you the rundown as my sources have relayed it. I know you started working as a junior swim instructor at Camp Sound View. I know you made some new friends there, with whom you came to spend a great deal of time. I know you were involved with a very successful Patrol This trial program with Arnie. I know your family found the house of their realistic dreams and were ready to pack their bags and say *adios* to peeling paint and rusty appliances forever." Aunt Violetta paused. "How am I doing?"

"Fine," Maggie mumbled.

"Good. I also know your parents are upset that you've refused to go to Camp Sound View in two weeks. I know you spent less time with your old friends as you spent more time with your new friends. I know you've missed three Patrol This meetings. I know the deal fell through on the house." Aunt Violetta paused. When she spoke again, her voice was softer. "And I know you haven't resorted to chocolate in a very, very long time."

"You forgot something." Silent tears rolled down Maggie's cheeks. She reached into the pocket of her hooded sweatshirt and grabbed a miniature Peanut Butter Cup.

"What's that?"

"That it's never going to be enough," she said around the candy.

"What's never going to be enough, sugar?"

Maggie shoved the blanket to her waist, sat up, and shimmied until her back pressed against the headboard. "Here's what I know. After the most horrible year of my life, in which I morphed into some monster-like creature weighing nearly two hundred pounds, I worked *so* hard, night and day, through muscle aches and hunger pains, to become a normal person again. Which I did, or at least I thought."

"Sweetie, you're—"

"I liked a boy, Aunt Violetta. I mean, *really* liked him.

I counted down the minutes until I could see him at our lockers, I looked forward to the end of the weekend because that meant Monday—and the chance to see him—was hours away, I kept a photo montage of him taped to my nightstand." She leaned forward to open the nightstand drawer and show Aunt Violetta the stack of photos, which she'd immediately removed after Peter had rejected her. "I never wanted to be the kind of girl who had a photo montage of a boy taped to any piece of furniture, but I was, because *that's* how much I liked him." She shut the drawer and flopped back against the headboard.

"So what happened?"

Maggie covered her face with one hand. "I was an idiot."

"I doubt that."

"No, really." She uncovered her face. "After months of wishing we were more than friends, I finally asked him out. *Me!* Asking out a boy. It was a terrible idea from the start."

"Which you wouldn't have followed through on if you didn't really want to, and there's nothing wrong with that."

"Anyway, he said no, of course—I don't know if I'd ever really thought he'd say anything else. And I was devastated. I lay on the couch and watched bad daytime TV for days before Mom basically enlisted me at Camp Sound View.

And I swore off boys for the rest of the summer, because there was no way I was going through that again."

"Sounds logical."

"But *then* I met another boy. Whom I didn't initially think of as a boy, because I wasn't thinking about boys in general, but whom I gradually got to know and who, for some reason, seemed to like me. And this boy was older, adorable, smart, and nice—not to mention the most popular instructor at camp. Never in a million years would I have ever thought he'd like someone like me—"

"Someone like you being a brilliant, beautiful, talented girl."

"But he did. We hung out, alone and with his friends. I went to parties and bought new clothes. I sang karaoke in front of thirty people! For the first time ever, I felt like the girl I always wanted to be but never thought was possible. And that felt incredible." Maggie shoved her hands into the pockets of her hooded sweatshirt and looked at her lap.

"Sounds pretty good," Aunt Violetta said gently.

"Too good to be true." She sighed and looked to the ceiling. "It didn't mean anything. They found out who I used to be, took one look at some bad pictures, and bolted." They hadn't physically bolted after looking at the photos—she had—but they hadn't bothered to call once during the past two weeks, which meant the same thing.

"This world is filled with all types of people, lamb chop. Sounds like you just stumbled onto a fickle lot."

"And the worst part is that my real friends, the people who were my friends before, during, and after the phase of really bad photos, are no longer talking to me." The tears that had been pooling in her eyes suddenly spilled over. "So now I have nothing. No friends, no new house, nothing."

"It sounds like an unfortunate run."

"An unfortunate run? More like an unfortunate life. I'll *never* be the girl I want to be. My embarrassing past will always get in the way."

"Everyone has a past, sugar. And if those kids haven't lived the embarrassing part of theirs yet, they will. I promise."

Maggie sniffed and looked at the plastic bags and wrappers blanketing the floor. "I can't believe I ate all this candy."

"Don't worry about it—comfort food's okay every now and then. It's temporary, though, and you need a more permanent fix." Aunt Violetta looked around the room. "Do you have a computer in here, or did it get sucked up in the hurricane?"

"On the desk, under the Butterfingers and Baby Ruths."

Aunt Violetta reached into her purse. "Here."

Maggie took the paper bookmark. "www.PatrolThis.com."
She looked at Aunt Violetta. "You think I've lost my way so
much that I need weight-loss tips from the website I helped
create?"

"I think you could use some friendly direction."

Maggie pouted.

"Emphasis on 'friendly.'" Aunt Violetta smiled, patted
Maggie's knee, and stood up. "I believe the next Patrol This
meeting starts in an hour. I'd be happy to give you a ride."

Maggie tossed the bookmark on the nightstand and slid
back under the covers.

"Oh, and sugar?" Aunt Violetta was halfway through the
door when she turned back around. "Real friends see each
other through the hard times."

Maggie waited for Aunt Violetta to close the door and
retreat down the hallway before she flung off the blankets
and crawled out of bed. Socks, T-shirts, pajamas, and bags
of candy joined the mess on the floor as she cleared off
her laptop. She pushed another load of clothes off her desk
chair, plopped down, and tried to ignore the waistband of
her jeans gently digging into her waist for the first time in
months.

She hadn't been to the Patrol This website since she'd left
Arnie's laptop with the lake house housekeeper on her way

home from the fateful Stella's shopping spree. She closed her eyes and braced herself as the site loaded, preparing herself for the worst-case scenario of her photo slideshow front and center on the home page.

She counted to ten before opening one eye, then the other. When she saw Arnie's face smiling at her in a small cartoon television in the middle of an otherwise empty black screen, she couldn't help but smile back. She clicked on the miniature play button, and smiled wider as Arnie started talking.

"Hi, guys. I know what you're thinking—TV on a website about health, nutrition, and other boring stuff? Shouldn't I be looking at a picture of a fruit bowl, or some unnaturally happy people playing tennis? If my parents walk by, won't they think I'm just wasting time?" Arnie leaned closer and looked around like someone might be listening before facing the camera and whispering, "Here's the first lesson of Weight Loss 101: It's about you, not them."

The small TV faded out and the main page filled the screen. Maggie's eyes filled with tears again as she recognized the photo that had apparently replaced the one in which she'd resembled a walrus in the screen's upper-left corner. Aimee had taken it when they were hanging at Arnie's lake house a few weeks before school let out. In it, Maggie and Arnie sat at the edge of the dock, their legs dangling over the side, with their backs to the camera. She remembered they'd been in a heated debate over who had better stage-side manner—Oprah, Ellen, or Dr. Phil—and that Maggie had laughed so hard, she almost fell in the lake. She could tell she was laughing when Aimee took the picture, because her head was tilted back.

She hadn't laughed like that in a long time.

She went through the entire site, clicking on recipes, different music playlists for different exercises, and more video blogs of Arnie struggling to make his chin touch the floor while doing push-ups, having trouble boiling water to make whole wheat pasta, and racing his neighbor's poodle to the end of the block—and losing. (The general theme of the video blogs seemed to be that it didn't matter if you didn't quite succeed at whatever you tried as long as you tried, which was very wise while being very Arnie-appropriate.) The only thing she skipped over was her photo slideshow, which was listed right under Arnie's. She was about to watch him do another set of pushups when she noticed a flashing spiral notebook at the bottom of the page.

Arnie's Online Diary, or, How Food Got in the Way Today.

Maggie clicked on the notebook.

> *Dear Maggie,*
>
> *Had a bad experience with a vending machine today.*

It's really my flute teacher's fault—he moved his studio from his house to a strip mall, forcing me to go from no snack before dinner to which *snack before dinner. Anyway, there I was, standing in front of a shiny glass case filled with candy, cookies, peanuts, and chips, trying to decide whether I was really going to try to be good, or treat myself just once, to celebrate my flute teacher's relocation—sort of like a house-warming gift to myself. And I put in three quarters, and was about to hit B8—Cracker Jack—and I thought of you. Not because caramel-coated popcorn usually makes me think of you—though maybe the idea of the prize inside does. Anyway, for whatever reason, I thought of you, and everything we've accomplished and been through together, and I decided to walk away from the vending machine. I even let it keep my three quarters instead of getting breath mints or gum. Because I don't want to be tempted like that. I don't want to lose to a vending machine ever again.*

Another fine example of you making things better, even when you're not there.

Till tomorrow's tasty trial,

Arnie

Maggie closed the entry and opened the one from the day before. And the day before that. And every day of the entire week before that.

He had written to her in every one.

A steady stream of tears had traveled down her cheeks since the first "Dear Maggie". After reading the entries, she wiped her eyes with her sweatshirt sleeves and clicked on the small MMT icon in the bottom right corner of the screen.

She held her breath until *Maggie's Master Multi-Tasker* popped up, and then exhaled in relief. There was no reason for it to have disappeared—lack of use didn't usually erase a document—but she felt better immediately, like as long as the spreadsheet still existed, then so did the chance that she could get her life back on track. She clicked on a new tab and quickly made five additions.

1. *Stop eating chocolate.*

2. *Clean room (and throw out any remaining chocolate).*

3. *Apologize a million times to Aimee.*

4. *Apologize a million times to Arnie.*

5. *Don't ever, EVER forget what—and who—really matters.*

She saved the changes, pushed the laptop aside, and dug through her desk drawer for a pen and empty notebook.

It was a long shot, but if Aunt Violetta was right, if real friends saw through the hard times, she had to try.

24. Maggie leaned against the wall just inside the classroom. No one had spotted her yet, because everyone—kids, parents, Arnie, and even Electra—was too busy dancing, jumping, and kicking to Gwen Stefani to pay attention. She'd been there since the beginning of the song and Maggie still couldn't figure out what was going on. From their place in the front of the room, Lucy and Paolo seemed to provide some kind of direction (when they punched the air, the rest of the group punched the air; when they did cartwheels, the rest of the group sort of put their hands on the floor and jumped), though it was still hard to be sure since they tended to burst into giggles every three seconds. Whatever they were doing, there was no doubt they were having a great time doing it.

"Awesome job!" Arnie exclaimed when the song ended

and everyone stopped bouncing long enough to clap and cheer. "Thanks to Lucy and Paolo for their creative choreography. Please join us next week for part four of our Rock Superstar series, as Margo and Alex get us sweating to . . . ?"

"50 Cent!" Alex pumped both fists in the air as Margo shook her head and buried her face in her hands.

"Interesting," Arnie said. "Okay, that's a wrap, guys. Check out the website, eat a lot of spinach, and have a great week."

Maggie hung back as the kids and parents prepared to leave. They definitely lingered longer than they used to, talking, laughing and making plans for the kids to get together during the week. And the positive environment was clearly doing more than fostering healthy socialization and play dates; Margo's adorable cheeks were smaller, Alex's little belly was flatter, and Paolo's favorite T-shirt, the one he wore to every meeting, was looser. The kids were having fun *and* losing weight.

She'd already felt bad for missing meetings, but now her stomach flip-flopped for not being there to congratulate the kids on their great progress. What if it was too late? What if they'd forgotten all about her—or worse, didn't forgive her for disappearing?

"Maggie!"

Hannah charged across the room, and the rest of the kids followed close behind. Before Maggie could brace for impact, they surrounded her in a big, sloppy group hug. She didn't know why, but they all seemed happy to see her.

"Where've you been?"

"Where'd you go?"

"We missed you!"

"Hi, guys! You all look amazing!" Maggie's eyes filled with tears for the trillionth time that afternoon. She didn't deserve the warm reception, and vowed to never disappoint them again. "I just had to take a little break, but I'm back now." She looked up to silently ask Arnie if that was really true—if he would even want her back after she'd just vanished without explanation.

"Give Maggie some air, people," Arnie called across the room. "You can bombard her with questions next week."

Next week.

Maggie smiled at Arnie, but he quickly turned away and started cleaning up the snack table.

The parents graciously welcomed her back as they hustled the kids out of the classroom. Electra did the same, and gave her a big hug. It was much more than she'd expected or deserved. She was thrilled, but knew winning over the person who mattered most wouldn't be so easy.

She waited by the door until she and Arnie were the only ones in the classroom.

"It's working," she offered gently.

The empty water bottle he tossed made a loud *thwack* as it hit the metal garbage can.

"They're having fun, making friends, and losing weight. Their whole lives are changing for the better because of you."

"Not just me," he grumbled, gathering leftover carrot sticks.

She paused. "I visited the website. I hit every link, watched every video blog, and read every message on the message board. It's amazing. People all over the country are really responding."

"It's getting ten times the hits the company anticipated," Arnie said. His back was still to her, but his voice wasn't as gruff.

"And I came up with something for the site. I mean, I totally understand if you want me completely hands-off—if you even want me back at all—so no worries if you don't post it." She took the notebook from her purse. "Can I run it by you?"

Sighing, Arnie turned toward her, leaned against the snack table, and crossed his arms over his chest. "I'm listening."

It was music to her ears. She opened the notebook to the carefully written note that she'd attempted on three pieces of scrap paper first. *Maggie's Online Journal, or How I Got in the Way Today.* She glanced up to see him staring at the floor. He didn't look happy, but he didn't look like he was about to stop her, either. "'Dear Arnie. I had a bad encounter with myself today—and yesterday, and the day before that, and about a month before that. It was my own fault. I started a new job where I met some people I thought were really cool. They asked me to hang out with them after work, and somehow I slowly became part of their group. I know it'll sound silly, and please forgive me for it being true—but I was in the popular crowd for the first time in my entire life, and I loved it. You know I'm all about books and studying, and that my good-student place is pretty permanently carved in stone at school. And you also know that last year, when I weighed 186 pounds, it was sometimes all I could do to get out of bed every day. So, when these older, funny, really great people wanted to hang out with me, it was a big deal. And I kind of got carried away.'" She paused.

"I'm still listening," he said, still looking at the floor.

"'As it happened, these really great people, who I thought were my new friends, turned out to be not so great. Once they accidentally found out about my past, they acted like I was any other person walking down the street—they didn't care about me, or my feelings. And that hurt—a lot—but what was a million times worse was what I did myself. I was so caught up in this new exciting life, I became a completely different person—I cut my hair, spent a ton of money on clothes I never would've considered wearing before, and I hardly ate in front of a boy because I worried he might think I was eating too much and guess at who I used to be. All ridiculous, I know, but true.'"

"The haircut's cute, by the way."

"Thank you." Maggie smiled before continuing. "'But I hit an all-time low when I started neglecting my best friends— my *real* friends. I let myself believe I was just busy, that I'd catch up with them eventually and they'd understand when I did. I was extremely selfish, and I took them for granted. You can never be too busy for friends.'" She took a deep breath. "'I'm *so* sorry, Arnie. You're amazing, and I'm an idiot. And I wouldn't blame you if you never forgive me . . . but I hope you do. I promise I'll do anything I can to make things right. Till tomorrow, and forever yours, Maggie.'"

Arnie stared at the floor for a few seconds more before looking up. "I get it."

Maggie's heart lifted in her chest.

"I don't like it," he clarified, "but I get it."

"I'm a moron," she said, shaking her head and stepping toward him. "The biggest moron in the history of moronic behavior."

"You could've called."

"I know."

"Or e-mailed."

"I know."

"Or sent smoke signals."

"Really?"

"You could've talked to me, Maggie. After everything we've been through together, you know I would've understood. Or at least listened and tried to understand."

"I know," she said, quieter.

"I only knew you were alive because Aunt Violetta has the gift of gab. She told Electra, who told me."

"Arnie, I'm so, so sorry."

"I know." He sighed. "And I'm not mad because of what you did—I mean, I am a little. But I'm mostly just upset and sad."

Maggie felt the familiar sting of fresh tears.

For the first time in weeks, his eyes met hers, and he smiled slightly. "This all," he said, nodding to the classroom, "is going *so* well. Our little summer project that we didn't ask for and weren't even sure we wanted when we got it, is a big hit. The company couldn't be more thrilled."

"That's great," Maggie said sincerely.

"It is, but it's been hard to enjoy it without you. It's *our* thing, you know?"

"Is it still our thing?" she asked hopefully. "It's not too late for me to be a part of it?"

His smile grew as he left the snack table and headed for the teacher's desk at the front of the classroom. He pulled two long white envelopes from the front pocket of his laptop bag, and held one out to her.

"What's this?" She joined him at the desk and took the envelope.

"Proof."

Not sure what that was supposed to mean, she lifted the envelope flap and peered inside. "A check?" She pulled the blue slip from the envelope—and leaned herself against the desk when her knees gave. She looked at him, at the check, and back at him. "This is a joke."

"When it comes to their money, corporations don't mess around."

Maggie stared at the long black number printed on the check. "There are three zeros," she said incredulously.

"With another digit in front of them."

"Arnie," she said, needing confirmation that she wasn't imagining things, "this check is for a thousand dollars." The most money she'd ever had at any one time—since her parents' seemingly limitless credit card didn't count—was when she'd won twenty dollars on an instant lottery ticket Aunt Violetta bought her.

"Yup."

She looked at him. "And my name's on it."

"Right again."

"But… *why*?"

"Our local Patrol This trial has been so successful in such a short amount of time, the Pound Patrollers corporation plans to expand the program—slowly to start, with two more locations in our area, and then more from there, depending on how it goes. But they want us to stay involved. These checks are a sort of 'thank-you' bonus, with a 'please continue' attached."

Maggie shook her head, not quite believing what she was hearing. "What do we have to do?"

"Participate in weekly meetings, update the website, and maybe make a few appearances around the area. Basically what we've been doing, with a few mini–road trips thrown in for kicks."

Maggie slid the check back in the envelope and held it toward Arnie.

"What's wrong?"

"What we've been doing is what *you've* been doing. I'm

not at all responsible for the early success of Patrol This." She shook the check gently. "I can't take this."

"Maggie," he said. "So what if you've been lying a little low lately? Without you, I never would've lasted at Pound Patrollers. And if I hadn't lasted at Pound Patrollers, I never would've lost the weight that I did. And if we hadn't been the charmingly dynamic duo that we are—the two of us, together—we never would've been asked to be involved with this project. It took both of us to get here, and it'll take both of us to keep going. You deserve the money."

Maggie lowered her outstretched arm and looked at the envelope. She didn't know if what Arnie said was true, or if he was just being his usual kind, generous self. In any case, regardless of whether she deserved the money, one thing was certain. "I won't let you down," she promised softly.

"I know." He smiled and flopped in the chair behind the teacher's desk. "Now how about we post that journal entry on *our* website?"

Beaming, Maggie pulled up a chair. One thousand dollars was a ton of money that could buy a ton of things (all of which she would certainly contemplate and list as soon as she got home). But right then, nothing—not one thousand dollars, not one billion dollars—was worth more than sitting next to Arnie.

25.

According to the bathroom scale at home, Maggie's post-traumatic candy binge had set her back six pounds. Not a huge amount in the grand scheme of lifelong weight fluctuation, but enough to make her feel like she was towing a small child as she swam a seventh lap. Refusing to quit before finishing ten laps, she slowed her pace, but forced her arms and legs to keep moving. When she was done, she treaded briefly before heading for shore.

"Oh," Ben said, dropping his bottle of sunscreen as she neared the beach. "Maggie. I didn't realize that was you out there."

The swim had served its purpose of alleviating some of the nervousness she'd felt returning to camp for the first time in two weeks, and she managed to make it out of the water without tripping and falling. "Hi, Ben," she said, forcing a polite smile.

"Hi." He looked at her and opened his mouth to speak. When nothing came out, he bought time by bending over to retrieve the sunscreen.

She grabbed her towel and wrapped it around her waist. She'd heard Ben's and Jason's laughter around lap five, and glanced toward the beach just long enough to see them emerging from the camp trail. She'd expected them to be there for their early morning workout (which was why she'd arrived an hour earlier, to beat them and boost her confidence with a good swim), and was prepared for the inevitable awkward conversation.

"How's it going?" he asked, smiling as though it were just another day. "You've been pretty busy, huh?"

"Very." She leaned to one side and squeezed excess water from her hair. "And you?"

"Insanely busy, actually."

"Hey, look who it is!" Finishing his beach sprints, Jason ran toward them. "Good to see you, Maggie."

"Thanks." She lifted her backpack from the sand and headed toward the lifeguard stand. "See you guys later. Have a good swim."

She knew they probably were looking at her as she walked

away, and then at each other, confused, but she kept going without turning around. She focused only on the stand, and once she reached it, did her best to block out any image of her and Ben huddling and talking together during the lightning storm. Seeing him again stung even more than she'd anticipated, but right then, she had more important things to worry about.

She sat in the sand and pulled a notebook from her backpack. She wanted to make sure she included every single detail for that day's Patrol This online journal entry.

> *Dear Arnie,*
>
> *I'm nervous. I know we talked things out and evaluated every possible scenario. I know you said everything would work out and be fine, and I know you're usually right. But as I sit on the beach with "the cool kids" only a few feet away, my heart's racing and my palms are sweating, and I'm wondering if you might be wrong on this one. If, for some miraculous reason, this all does have a happy ending, it'll be because I forced myself to swim ten whole laps—quite an achievement after not exercising and after living on sugar for weeks, and proof that bouncing back is possible. Honestly, I don't know how I got through life before Aimee got me in the pool.*

The last sentence was especially true and an appropriate one to temporarily end on, so she capped her pen and swapped the notebook for e-mail correspondence between Arnie, Electra (who would continue to be the official adult Patrol This leader), and regional Pound Patrollers execs regarding future expansion plans. He'd printed everything out for her so she'd be all caught up. She was in the middle of a note about proposed Patrol This merchandise—baseball hats, beach towels, pillowcases and, of course, T-shirts—when she heard the familiar snippy voice she'd been waiting for.

"Nice vacation?"

Maggie shoved the papers in her backpack and jumped up. "Hi, Erin."

She stood in front of the stand, hugging her clipboard and eyeing Maggie warily. "I hope you brought back souvenirs."

"Just me, sorry." Maggie tried to laugh. When Erin's stony expression remained unchanged, she plowed ahead. "Erin, I'm really sorry for the past two weeks. Something came up—which is no excuse for not calling or letting you know, I know—but believe me, I'm here now, and for the long haul."

"You're fired, you know."

Maggie's mouth fell open, then snapped shut. She'd

mentally prepared for that response, but hadn't anticipated it coming so soon into her apology.

"You fail to report to work, give your sister the unsavory chore of explaining that you haven't been feeling well, and then just show up here two weeks later, expecting me to welcome you back with open arms?"

"Absolutely not." Maggie swallowed. "I mean, I don't expect anything. I just—"

"But you're here because you want your job back."

"Yes." Maggie paused. "And I want to work with you."

Erin shook her head, as if by jostling the request, it might make more sense. "Why?"

Maggie glanced toward the water as Jason and Ben came bounding out. "I just do, that's all."

Erin looked behind her to see what had caught Maggie's attention. When she turned back, her expression was softer. "And how do I know you won't fall off the planet again next week?"

"Because," Maggie said firmly, jumping on the chance to continue her belated—if inadequate—explanation, "I was kind of pushed off the planet when I wasn't looking before, and there's no way I'm letting that happen again."

Sighing, Erin flipped through pages on her clipboard. "I'm not usually into second chances—and you should know there won't be a third, under any circumstances—but my campers can be monsters. I could use some help with my group—especially an extra set of lungs for disciplining." She scribbled on a loose piece of paper and handed it to Maggie. "You will be here every single day, on time, and do as I ask when I ask."

"Absolutely." Maggie looked at the list of names in disbelief. "Erin, thank you *so* much. You have no idea what this means."

"I think I do." Erin offered a sympathetic almost-smile. "I was pushed off the planet when I wasn't looking once, myself." Her walkie-talkie squealed suddenly, and she hurried away from Maggie as she snatched it from the waistband of her shorts.

The moment was over as soon as it had begun, but it had happened. Maggie had her job back.

She flopped in the sand and worked on committing her campers' names to memory until the first groups descended on the beach. Their arrival marked the beginning of the second phase of her big plan, which actually made her much more nervous than she'd been prior to seeing Ben and Jason again.

The Figure Eights hit the beach in a flurry of squeals and giggles. Their close-knit happiness was a little intimidating, but Maggie shuffled toward them, determined.

"Hey, Maggie," Ben said, suddenly standing in front of her. "Do you have a second?"

"Um, not really." She looked past him, trying to keep Aimee in sight.

"I just thought maybe I could explain what happened. I'm guessing you saw us looking at your laptop after you came out of Stella's that night. I swear we turned it on just to try to check flight prices to New York for the weekend trip we'd been talking about, and then sort of saw the slideshow. We were totally wrong to even touch the computer, let alone look at your personal stuff, and I'm so sorry about that. And you're probably wondering why I haven't called, and—"

"Actually, I'm not wondering that at all," Maggie said pleasantly. "But maybe we can catch up later?"

She knew this was probably his one shot at trying to clear the air, but this might be hers, too, with Aimee. And some things were just more important. She'd wonder later what he could've possibly said, but apologized quickly before continuing her dash across the sand.

"Hi."

Aimee spun around, her giggle instantly fading when she realized who'd spoken. "Maggie. What're you doing here?"

"I work here." Maggie tried to smile, but it was hard to do with Aimee looking so mad.

"I thought you *used* to work here? Summer said you were taking some time off?"

Maggie peered past Aimee to the other Figure Eights watching them curiously. "Can we talk? Please?"

Aimee frowned and crossed her arms over her chest, but shuffled after Maggie when Maggie moved away from the gathering groups. "What's up?" she asked when they were safely out of eavesdropping range.

"How are you?" Maggie was careful to not respond in the same curt tone.

Aimee looked at her, apparently thrown off by the question.

"I see you're Queen of the Day again."

"Not again," Aimee said, adjusting the tiara. "Still."

"Still? But you were Queen of the Day weeks ago."

"I guess I'm good at it."

"I guess," Maggie said doubtfully. "Or else you keep beating out everyone else for the throne."

Aimee shrugged and looked down to her bare feet.

"Aim," Maggie said gently. "How do you keep beating out everyone else for the throne?"

"Forget it."

"Aimee, please—"

"Maggie, what do you care?" Aimee looked around quickly, apparently realizing how loudly she'd spoken. When she spoke again, her voice was still harsh, but quieter. "I mean, you started working here and were instantly too cool for anyone else, and then you started dating some stupid guy and disappeared for weeks. Weeks! And now you just show up and expect me to chat like nothing happened?"

"Aimee, I know. And I'm sorry. So sorry. I'm an idiot. A moron. A loser. I don't deserve you to speak to me now, but I just want you to know that I do care. And I know something's up and I'm so sorry I wasn't there for you before, but I am now, and I will be later, if you'll let me, and—"

"My parents are getting divorced, okay?"

Maggie gasped. After replaying every weird conversation they'd had in recent weeks and leaving a dozen more unreturned messages, Maggie had finally decided something was definitely wrong with Aimee, but she never would've expected that. Aimee's parents always seemed so happy. Growing up, Maggie had wished more than once that her own parents could be more like them.

"Listen, I don't really feel like talking about it, and I have to get back—"

Maggie threw her arms around Aimee and squeezed. "You don't have to talk now if you don't want to. But know that I'm so sorry, Aim. And whenever you do want to talk, I'm here to listen."

Aimee's body stiffened slightly before she gave in and hugged Maggie back. "I'm sorry too. It's just been a lot to deal with. And I felt like I was losing you while I was losing my family, and I was just, well, *mad*, you know?"

"I know," Maggie said, still hugging Aimee.

"And I didn't really push to talk to you, even though I know I would've felt so much better if I did."

"But I know you tried. And I know I was too wrapped up in my own silliness to notice." Maggie paused. "Do you want to sleep over tonight? We can stay up really late talking? And hopefully laughing? And maybe crying, if we need to?"

Still hugging, Aimee nodded against Maggie's shoulder.

"I've missed you, Aim."

"Me too." Aimee sniffed.

When they finally pulled away to head to their separate groups, Maggie found herself thinking of her online journal entry to Arnie. She'd have lots of details to add, but already knew the last lines.

> *You were right once again, Arnie—everything's going to be fine. Another fine example of you making things better, even when you're not there.*

26.

"Where's the spinach dip?"

Maggie looked up from the cutting board to see her mom flying around the kitchen, throwing open the refrigerator, drawers, and cabinets.

"And the broccoli puffs? And the strawberry spread?"

"Mom." Maggie waited for her to stop spinning and make eye contact. When she did, Maggie pointed the knife she was using to cut peppers at the platter in front of her. "You put them there two minutes ago."

"Thank goodness." Her mom sighed in relief. "New space, new layout. I guess I'm still adjusting."

"Not a bad situation to have to adjust to," Summer said. She sat at the breakfast table, tying ribbons around bundles of plastic utensils.

"Not at all." Her mother beamed and fanned her eyes as they filled with their daily dose of tears.

"Good news!" Her dad entered the kitchen wearing a crisp white apron, red oven mitts, and a PATROL THIS baseball hat. He placed a plate holding a single turkey burger on the counter. "Not only does the new grill work, I actually seem to know how to use it."

"That *is* good news," Maggie said, impressed.

"Especially since the guests will be arriving any minute," her mom said sweetly before planting a kiss on her dad's cheek and dashing from the room—to nervously rearrange the outdoor seating again, most likely.

"And here we are in barbecue headquarters."

"Not again," Summer groaned playfully as Arnie came into the kitchen. "Don't you ever put that thing down?"

"You'll get your interview later, missy," Arnie said, aiming the digital camcorder in her direction. "Now, what's this?"

"A turkey burger," Maggie's dad said proudly.

"Not bad. Lower in fat than regular hamburgers." Arnie zoomed in on the plate before moving to the end of the counter for another close-up. "But there's still potential trouble ahead."

"Mustard?" Summer asked skeptically.

"Fixings, in general. This is where ninety percent of calorie counters' mistakes are made at barbecues. Mustard isn't so bad. But ketchup, very deceiving in its tomato origin, is full of sugar. Couple that with some thick slices of cheddar cheese and fatty rolls, and one burger has your day's entire calorie allotment."

"Okay." Maggie added the last pepper slices to a dish, wiped her hands on a kitchen towel, and reached across the counter to gently turn the camcorder toward her. "How about we take a little break?"

"But this thing can go on for hours. Its battery life—"

"Help me decide what to wear," she called over her shoulder, already out the kitchen door.

"Sweetie."

Maggie turned to see her mother coming at her with outstretched arms. Before she could joke about her bruised ribs, a result of her mother's nonstop spontaneous hugging, she was swept up in another squeeze.

"I got that just before powering off," Arnie whispered after her mother released her and flew back into the kitchen. He tapped the camcorder.

"Sorry about the skyrocketing emotional levels," Maggie said, heading down the hallway to her bedroom. "Mom's been a basket case for weeks, all through the closing, packing, and moving, but she's been kind of out of control the past few days. This is the first housewarming party we've ever had. Actually, this is probably the first real party of any kind we've ever had, outside of Summer's and my birthdays."

"It's a big deal. Based on what you've told me, compared to where you were a year ago, your family's kind of starting over."

She opened her closet and smiled slightly. It was true. They were all starting over. Shortly after their mortgage fell through, Ocean Vista Pools made an enormous deal with Meadowbrook Estates, the ever-expanding neighborhood where they'd fallen in love with the astronomically priced blue Colonial; when the builder behind the complex was looking for another pool company to outfit new neighborhood backyards, her dad somehow convinced Wilma, their original realtor, that she owed it to them to put in a good word for his company. Ocean Vista got the gig and a ton more work, her dad got a bonus for influencing the deal, and their family got the down payment they needed for the white ranch house.

And Maggie had done some starting over of her own. After mentally processing the fact that she had one thousand dollars, a great deal of money that could buy lots of books—now, or even later, if she put it away for college—she eventually gave it all to her parents. Most of it paid off her impulsive Stella's shopping spree (the purchases from which she'd kept for a Patrol This contest prize) before her parents received the credit card bill and grounded her for life, and the rest she'd suggested they put toward their housewarming party. She'd also conducted daily apologies for her odd behavior, brief bout of materialism, and sneaking around to meet her now-ex-friends, until her parents grew so tired of hearing her, they reminded her once again that she was only thirteen years old, and therefore subject to all sorts of odd behavior and mistakes. Which, of course, didn't make any of it okay—but it at least made it somewhat understandable. She didn't know if they really believed that or if they were just too happy to punish her; either way, she hadn't stayed out late or bought anything since.

"What do you think?" She spun around and held up two sundresses.

"They're both great," Arnie said, sitting in the chair of her wide white desk. "And since this is such a big deal, maybe you can just change halfway through? Like at the Oscars?"

"I'll go with the blue. It's long, frilly, and gets bonus points for matching my room."

"That certainly affects my outfit selection every morning."

"Speaking of your room," Maggie said, flopping on her

new full-size bed across from Arnie. "How're things at Casa Gunderson? Aren't your parents back from Rome?"

"They are indeed. And things have been..." He paused. "Interesting."

"'Interesting' sounds better than 'painful.'"

"It is. Turns out they found out about our little project."

"But you vowed never to tell them anything about Patrol This, so they couldn't tell you how you were doing everything all wrong?"

"I didn't tell them—the housekeeper found my bonus check on my desk when she was cleaning my room. I gave them a website tour when they brought it up, and they actually asked legitimate questions and seemed pretty impressed. My dad even shook my hand—his hug equivalent—afterward."

"Arnie, that's wonderful!"

"Yeah. I still don't see them much, but when I do, we talk about the site, or business, in general. It's not an ideal parent-son relationship, but it's better than them yelling and me cowering. It's a start."

"I'm so happy for you. Soon you'll be able to teach them a thing or two."

"I don't know about that."

Hearing the doorbell ring, Maggie jumped up from the bed. "I should finish getting ready."

"Right." Arnie jumped up from the desk chair.

Maggie took the blue dress from its hanger and retrieved her silver flip-flops from the closet.

"So, I should go."

"Probably." Maggie smiled.

"Um . . ."

When the doorbell rang again, announcing the arrival of more guests, Maggie looked at Arnie, who hadn't moved since standing. "Everything okay?"

"I kind of got you something."

"Got me something?"

He pulled a small box from the pocket of his khaki shorts. "It's a housewarming gift."

"Arnie, your parents already sent my parents the fanciest, most expensive crystal vase I've ever seen. You didn't have to do this."

He held the box toward her and smiled.

Smiling, she placed her dress and flip-flops on the bed and took the box. It was so pretty, wrapped in shiny blue paper with a matching silk ribbon, she almost didn't want to open it. "Aren't you going to get this on camera?"

"Nope. I want to watch you with my own eyes, not through a lens."

"Arnie!" She gasped when she unwrapped and opened

the box to reveal a delicate silver bracelet. "It's gorgeous. You really shouldn't have."

"I know it's not a typical housewarming gift," he said quickly. "It's not, like, wineglasses or an ice bucket. But the center stone's aquamarine, because you love water and swimming, and I thought silver would look good in any room in the house."

Maggie slid the bracelet on and held out her arm to admire it. "It's amazing." And it really was. No one had ever given her such a gift. She crossed the room and threw her arms around his neck. "Thank you *so* much."

"You're welcome." He paused briefly before hugging her back.

"Are you wearing cologne again?" she teased.

He pulled away gently. "Maggie."

"What's wrong?"

"Nothing." He looked at his feet, then at her. "I just don't know if you'll get it if I don't actually say it out loud."

"Get what?" she asked, concerned. He was suddenly so serious.

"Maggie, Aimee and Peter are here!" Summer called from the living room.

Still looking at Arnie, Maggie waited for the once reflexive flip-flopping of her stomach at the mention of Peter's name. A few weeks ago she'd decided that since she wasn't changing schools and would have to see him at their lockers every day again very soon, she had no choice but to accept and get over everything that had happened in the beginning of the summer. So she'd organized a mini-golf outing with him, Aimee, and Arnie. She was so nervous during the first five holes the mini–golf club repeatedly slid from her sweaty grip, but by the sixth hole, when Arnie hit his ball right into the ice-cream cone of a little girl nine holes away and they all laughed until they cried, everything was somehow okay. They'd all hung out several times since, and her stomach had seemed less jumpy with every visit.

Now, she couldn't help but smile slightly when her stomach growled (for turkey burgers, most likely) instead of flip-flopped.

"Sorry," Arnie said. "You should get ready."

"Arnie." Maggie grabbed his hand as he started to walk away. "What is it?"

"I like you," he finally said without looking at her. "I've liked you forever, and I haven't said anything because I was too scared and didn't know if you'd feel the same way. And I know you probably had no idea and that this probably seems like it's coming completely out of nowhere, but trust me—it's not. And I don't want to make anything weird or awkward, but

I just had to say something because if I didn't, someone else would've and I'd lose my chance. If I even have a chance."

Arnie spoke so quickly, Maggie had to really focus to make sure she caught every word. When she did, it took a second to process what he was actually saying.

Arnie liked her. As more than a friend.

She swallowed. "Well, that's—"

"You don't have to say anything now. Or ever, even. I just wanted you to know."

Arnie, one of her best friends, who understood what she'd been through the past year better than anyone, who made her laugh until her sides hurt and who would do anything for her, *liked* her. He was right—she hadn't expected it. But only because she'd been so busy obsessing about other things (and people) that she hadn't really thought about it. But now that she did, it didn't take long for the idea to make perfect sense. She didn't know if she deserved his affection, but if she didn't yet, she quickly, silently vowed to do everything she could until she did.

"You have a chance," she said gently, still holding his hand.

He looked at her and smiled. "Really?"

Returning his smile, she felt her cheeks burn. "Thank you for giving me one."

The doorbell rang again, and again.

"I guess you really need to get ready," he said, still smiling.

"I guess I do."

He squeezed her hand before letting it go. He grabbed the video camcorder from the desk, turned it on, and pointed the lens at himself. "Well, folks. It turns out there's much more to enjoy at Maggie's housewarming barbecue than turkey burgers and sugar-infused ketchup." He flashed her a quick grin, turned the camera away from himself, and left her to get dressed.

Standing in the middle of her new room, Maggie listened to the happy buzz of friends and family talking and laughing, and looked around at her lavender blue walls, book-lined shelves, and flowery duvet. As her eyes scanned the room, she caught the silver bracelet on her wrist in the reflection of her dresser mirror, and her heart flitted in her chest.

For once, everything was just as it should be.

She was home.